"Do you mind?"  **down her book**

"Mind what?" Cash grinned.

"Not undressing in front of me."

"In case you've forgotten, we might be strangers when it comes to knowing each other's favorite colors and foods. But in the biblical sense, back in Vegas, we pretty much became experts on each other's anatomy.

"It's all right, you know." He gave his chest and abs a flourish. "You're allowed to look."

Wren grabbed the nearest item of clothing from her suitcase and covered her eyes with it. "For the duration of my stay, it would be most appreciated if you'd disrobe in your private areas."

"Oh, honey, I'll keep my naked body behind closed doors, as long as you keep those scraps of lace you call panties off your face."

Yanking them down to see that she had indeed covered her eyes with underwear, she growled.

Cash took his sweet time, smiling all the way into the shower.

Dear Reader,

Through the magic of publishing, while you're reading this in December, I'm writing it in June. This month an event happened that I've been dreading for twelve years—my twins and bonus son graduated from high school. Where did the time go? I don't feel any different, yet the same kids I made smiley-face pancakes for and helped with their multiplication tables are now all of the sudden leaving home? *Noooooooooo!*

Meanwhile, as I spontaneously burst into tears during every diaper commercial, Hubby's elated. Don't get me wrong, he loves our brood as much as I do, but he views this situation in a dramatically different way. Once the buggers head off to college, he will never again find every towel in the house under our daughter's bed. No one will park in "his" spot. Most especially, random kids won't appear in our home at supper time to eat everything that isn't nailed down!

After twenty-two years of marriage, you would think Hubby and I are in sync on most issues. The truth is we're not even close—which is probably why we're still together. LOL!

Like Cash and Wren, we have our differences. Unlike them, our kids were very much planned and anticipated. "Cowboy" Cash is shocked by the news he's going to be a daddy, and the future big-city doctor carrying his child isn't faring much better. Wren's health crisis might temporarily force them together, but no force on Earth is strong enough to keep this stubborn duo from falling apart!

Merry Christmas!

Laura Marie

The Bull Rider's Christmas Baby

Laura Marie Altom

HARLEQUIN®

TORONTO • NEW YORK • LONDON
AMSTERDAM • PARIS • SYDNEY • HAMBURG
STOCKHOLM • ATHENS • TOKYO • MILAN • MADRID
PRAGUE • WARSAW • BUDAPEST • AUCKLAND

Recycling programs
for this product may
not exist in your area.

ISBN-13: 978-0-373-75340-6

THE BULL RIDER'S CHRISTMAS BABY

Printed in U.S.A.

ABOUT THE AUTHOR

After college (Go Hogs!), bestselling, award-winning author Laura Marie Altom did a brief stint as an interior designer before becoming a stay-at-home mom to boy/girl twins and a bonus son. Always an avid romance reader, she knew it was time to try her hand at writing when she found herself replotting the afternoon soaps.

When not immersed in her next story, Laura teaches art at a local middle school. In her free time, she beats her kids at video games, tackles Mount Laundry and of course reads romance!

Laura loves hearing from readers at either P.O. Box 2074, Tulsa, OK 74101, or email BaliPalm@aol.com.

Love winning fun stuff? Check out www.lauramariealtom.com!

Books by Laura Marie Altom

HARLEQUIN AMERICAN ROMANCE
1028—BABIES AND BADGES
1043—SANTA BABY
1074—TEMPORARY DAD
1086—SAVING JOE*
1099—MARRYING THE MARSHAL*
1110—HIS BABY BONUS*
1123—TO CATCH A HUSBAND*
1132—DADDY DAYCARE
1147—HER MILITARY MAN
1160—THE RIGHT TWIN
1165—SUMMER LOVIN'
       "A Baby on the Way"
1178—DANCING WITH DALTON
1211—THREE BOYS AND A BABY
1233—A DADDY FOR CHRISTMAS
1257—THE MARINE'S BABIES
1276—A WEDDING FOR BABY**
1299—THE BABY BATTLE**
1305—THE BABY TWINS**

 *U.S. Marshals
**Baby Boom

Belated congrats for my June graduates:
Terral Lynn Altom III, Hannah Marie Altom
& Russell Shook.

I'm not only crazy-proud of all of you,
but I can't wait to see what amazing grown-ups you
become! That said, no matter how old you may be,
you will always be my babies and as such,
are expected to forever believe in Santa, the
Easter Bunny and the wondrous healing powers
of a great big Mom hug! I love you!

Chapter One

Oklahoma rain drummed the rental car's roof, drowning out Hank Williams on the radio. For mid-September, the air was unbearably muggy. Feet swollen and the bagel she'd downed at Baltimore-Washington International threatening to make a break for it, Wren Barnes peered out her side window, praying she'd turned onto Cash Buckhorn's driveway and not merely another country road.

Thankfully, the drive stopped.

The downpour didn't.

Barely able to make out Cash's home through the rain, Wren prayed for the umpteenth time she'd made the right decision. Although regardless, there was no turning back now.

Since this would be a hasty mission, she'd leave her overnight bag on the passenger-side floorboard, but in case she needed tissues or antacid, she snatched her purse. Forcing a deep breath, she charged from her vehicle, running through the rain. Seconds later she stood on Cash's covered front porch, dripping.

Even in the midst of a storm, the home was lovely. A modern mix of stone walls and sheets of glass for windows. The place reeked of money, meaning as usual, she didn't fit in—would never fit in until she'd finished her training. But that was okay. She and her baby wouldn't be in Weed Gulch long. And then, back in Baltimore, the two of them would create the family she'd always craved.

Wren had just raised her hand to knock on a weathered copper-plated door when from around the corner stepped a cowboy and all that that implied. Through the steady downpour Wren couldn't get a complete image. Even squinting netted her the same sort of mouthwatering, wholly masculine, leather-chaps-wearing silhouette that had first gotten her into this mess. Mouth dry, pulse erratic, she managed to stammer, "C-Cash?"

"In the flesh, darlin'. What can I—" Having rounded the edge of an immaculate wildflower garden, he stepped onto the porch, not in the least concerned about the water dripping from his hat. "Oh. It's you."

The fact that her baby's father didn't even remember her name brought on a fresh wave of nausea. Bolting toward the rail, with as much grace as she could manage she upchucked the meal she'd tried so valiantly to keep down.

"Hey, whoa!" He stepped up behind her, taking firm hold of her heaving shoulders. "The gardener's gonna have my hide."

"S-sorry." Wren tried standing, but having had hardly any sleep for as long as she could remember, exhaustion clung like lead weights to her body.

"That's it," he soothed, tempting her to lean against the muscular chest forever seared into her memory. "Take it easy."

Never had she wished more that she was a delicate Southern belle prone to fainting. Alas, she'd been born in Philly to deadbeat parents. Forced from the tender age of two to survive in a church-run orphanage. The experience had delivered steady lessons in self-reliance. Because of which, she drew a deep breath, tugged her sweater over her nearly-six-month baby bump and refrained from any further leaning.

"You're Dr. Wren, right? We, ah, played your profession and then went on to dabble in mine?"

She cringed. Did he have to speak of such things in broad daylight? "Yes, um, unfortunately, that would be me."

"Well, hell, there wasn't anything unfortunate about that night. Unless you happened to catch a glance at our bar bill."

She'd forgotten his laugh. A slow, drawn-out chuckle of sorts during which he flashed strong white teeth and dimples in both of his whisker-stubbled cheeks. Cash wasn't merely handsome—with short, dirty-blond curls and eyes as green as daffodil stems, he was take-a-girl's-breath-away gorgeous. And he knew it. Confidence oozed from his every pore. Along with the knowledge that most every woman on the planet from age nine to ninety-two was helpless in the battle against his charm.

Except her. She'd already fallen once, and just as soon as she did the right thing in telling him he was going to be a father, she'd forever be on a *mostly* Cash-free diet.

"What's the matter?" he asked, removing his cowboy hat to whisk water droplets from leather chaps. Before seeing him ride bulls in that Vegas rodeo, she'd thought they'd been worn only in movies. "Missed me and thought you'd come round for more?"

"N-not exactly," she muttered. "I'm afraid it's more complicated. Would you mind going inside? I'm a little chilled."

"Sure." He opened the door and gestured for her to lead. He hadn't noticed her enormous belly, which, at the moment, suited her. The home was as spectacular on the inside as it was outside. With Native American motifs, buttery-soft leather sofas and lounge chairs placed around a soaring stone fireplace, she could only imagine how inviting it would be during a snow. Warm and cozy with a floor-to-ceiling view of rolling prairie and tumbling flakes. "Have a seat. Can I get you something to eat or drink?"

"No, thank you." Where to start? As wet as she was, she chose a wooden rocker.

He sat on the polished stone hearth. "Gotta say you're the last person I expected to see today."

"Yes, well, I—*we*—have had a problem arise." Not unlike her queasy stomach. "You might recall that when we, um, found pleasure on the balcony that the condom broke?"

"Oh, hell…" The tan slid from his face. "You're not tellin' me…"

"Cash, I'm pregnant with your baby." Before he got a grip on her last statement, she hit him with another. "But I'm not here to make demands—financial or otherwise." Curving her hands to her belly, she added, "If you'll recall, in Vegas I was celebrating my med-school graduation—the trip was a gift from a good friend—and was due to start residency in Baltimore mid-July. Well, as you can guess, this—"

"Ma'am, with all due respect, could you please stop yakking long enough to give a man time to think?"

"I'm chronically on the run. I don't have time to yak—more like hastily convey as-needed information."

Snorting, he said, "Hate to be the bearer of bad news, but honey, we've got a lot more to worry about than semantics."

"You think?" Standing, she paced, struggling to ignore the way the room had begun to spin.

"Being in your condition, shouldn't you sit? Better yet, get in bed?"

"Exercise is healthy." That said, her current degree of dizziness was not.

"Are you sure?" Though his expression seemed to hold genuine concern, it also held a fair amount of panic.

She nodded.

"Damn, I didn't see this coming." He'd taken a red bandanna from his back pocket and now wiped it across his forehead. "Yes, indeed, this does present some problems."

"But it doesn't have to. That's the beauty of my plan."

"Your plan?" He chuckled. "From where I'm sitting, looks like the bun in your oven is pulling our strings."

"Like I said, your life doesn't in any way need to change. I'm here on a fall break from my residency. I felt it best you hear this news in person. Now that you have, I'll be on my way and our baby no longer needs to be your concern."

He half laughed. "That's where you're wrong."

"Excuse me?"

"The baby growing inside you is a Buckhorn, and lady, I don't know diddly-squat about your family, but one thing you should know about mine is that our off-spring don't go anywhere until they're old enough to decide they want to."

Though she'd thankfully returned to her rocker, now he was the one pacing. "Yes, sirree, this does present a problem."

"Only if you let it." Her nausea and dizziness returned with a vengeance. Couldn't he be a gentleman and make this easy for her?

Slapping on his hat, he ambled with a slight limp toward the door.

"Where are you going?" she called, jumping to her feet. "We still have a lot to—"

Cash glanced back just in time to watch the very beautiful, very pregnant Wren Barnes crumple to the floor.

"You'll be fine," Doc Haven said to Wren thirty minutes later. She'd hardly budged since Cash had hefted her onto the sofa.

Cash thanked his lucky stars that the white-haired country doctor who'd been wearing the same wire-framed glasses since Cash was a little boy had been on a neighboring ranch when he'd called.

Checking her watch, Wren asked, "Does that mean I'm free to leave? It's a long drive back to Tulsa, and I've got a 5:00 a.m. flight."

"If that's the case," Doc said, rocking back on his heels, "we might have a situation."

"How so?" Wren wrinkled her pert nose. "I've got studying to do back home and am operating on a very narrow timeline."

"Sorry to hear that." After jotting a few notes in a

black journal, Doc said, "Your fainting spell and sky-rocketing blood pressure tell me you need to be off your feet for no less than a week before I'm clearing you to travel as far as the local feed store, let alone halfway across the country."

"I *am* leaving," Wren assured him, "and I would *never* faint."

Cash snorted. "Mind explaining why I had to scoop you up from the floor?"

Not meeting his gaze, she said, "I was tired. It's been a long day."

"Um-hmm." Doc wrote on a scratch pad, then tore off the top sheet and handed it to Cash. "I'll run tests on the blood and urine samples, and you head down to the pharmacy and pick her up some iron tabs. Call if anything changes. In the meantime, you two kids behave."

With the doctor gone, Wren struggled for the right thing to say. Not only had she planned to be headed home already, but she was stuck staying with a man she hardly knew? No. Easing upright on the sofa she said, "Now that we're on our own, if you'd be so kind as to help me to the door, I'll…" Hand to her forehead, she used every ounce of her strength to hold her spinning nausea at bay.

"Can it," Cash said, sliding his hands under her before lifting her into his arms.

She squeaked, automatically circling her arms around his neck. "Put me down."

"Why? So you can get yourself all riled up only to faint again? Not happening on my watch. You gave me a hell of a scare. For the next week, you just plan on keeping that luscious booty of yours in bed."

Reddening at the memory of his hands on her bare *booty,* she said, "But I have to get…"

With a long stride, he'd already headed down a shadowy hall, grunting as he veered to his right to enter a sumptuous bedroom. Featuring another wall of windows, this one overlooked a free-form pool and hot tub surrounded by low rock walls and more wildflowers that looked as if they'd always been there. Wheat-colored carpet cushioned his footfalls. A rough-hewn log bed had been made in down linens.

Cash set her on the bed as carefully as if she were a porcelain doll. At the moment, as wretched as she felt, she appreciated his help. Though admitting any sort of weakness had never been her strong suit, this was one case in which she felt as if her own body was betraying her. "Bathroom's in here," he said, laying a throw blanket over her before ducking through another door to flip on lights to bathroom luxury fit for a five-star spa. "After you've rested for a while, help yourself to whatever you need. There should be towels and spare toiletries. Food's in the fridge. I…" He sharply exhaled. "Sorry, this has all caught me off guard. I need to get out of here for a while. I've gotta have time to think."

"Sure," she said, casting him a faint smile. "I understand. Take all the time you need."

IN THE BARN, SURROUNDED by his favorite smells of oats, straw and horses, Cash dropped to sit hard on a hay bale, in the process jamming his screwed-up knee. He grimaced at the pain. If it hadn't been for a nasty spill he'd taken in Oklahoma City just three weeks prior and in the process tearing the medial collateral ligament, he wouldn't even be here. Pending further MRI readings, National Bull Rider tour docs had put him on a minimum six-week leave.

Taking out his phone, he hit speed dial for his big brother, Dallas. Though Cash was a respectable twenty-seven years old, on this particular afternoon he felt all of six, facing his father after having accidentally blown his math book to bits with a superstrength firecracker.

"What's up?" Dallas answered on the second ring. "Finish exercising the mares?"

"Yes, but—"

"And you got them in the barn before the storm?"

"Not yet, but—"

"Dammit, Cash, you're killing me. I know you've got a full plate, but we're trying to run a business here, and—"

Cash had never been what one might call an expert communicator, so before heartburn churned up his gut, he blurted out, "I'm pregnant."

"What?"

"Yeah. You know how Ruby dumped me right before that last ride I had in Vegas?"

"Uh-huh..." Even Dallas's grunts didn't sound happy.

"To celebrate, I hooked up with this uptight brunette from out East, only turns out she was actually pretty wild, and—"

"Holy hell," Dallas roared, "would you get to the damn point!"

"Condom broke. She's pregnant."

His big brother, the rock of their family since their father had died three years earlier, had apparently fallen speechless.

"You there?"

"Oh, I'm here, all right. When's the wedding? Mama

didn't raise us to not do right by a woman. If she catches wind of this before you put a ring on that gal's finger, you'll never hear the end of it."

"I know, which is why I'm calling. I realize everyone will expect me to do the so-called right thing, but what if I can't?"

"So help me, if this is one of your practical jokes…"

"Honestly, would I joke about something like this? Vegas was hot, but God's honest truth, right now I'd swear off women forever. Had my eye on a smoking-hot redhead that night in OK City when I took my fall. Should've had my mind on business. Females are nothing but trouble, and—"

"Would you hush? Your voice is bringing on a migraine. In the meantime, you need to reassess your marriage views before Mom gets wind of this."

"Thanks, bro. You've been a lot of help." Especially considering Cash hadn't even gotten around to telling his brother he was now stuck with the woman living in his home for an indefinite length of time.

Dallas grunted. "And my whole damned life you've been a walking—or in this case, limping—pain in my ass."

WREN RESTED ON HER SIDE, staring out the bedroom window, trying to regroup. She was drowning in fear. In hindsight, hopping a plane and showing up on Cash's doorstep hadn't been one of her brightest ideas. Should she have stayed in Baltimore? Told Cash he was going to be a father via internet or phone?

Eyes stinging, the ever-present knot in her throat hurting more than usual, she indulged in a brief crying jag before forcing a deep breath. Her entire life she'd been on her own. The orphanage had taught her to become an island. Self-sufficient and independent. Knowing she wanted more for her future family, she'd studied hard. Won scholarships. Fought her way to the top of her college and then med-school classes.

An unplanned pregnancy went against everything she'd fought so hard to become. That said, she hugged her womb, knowing that despite this momentary setback, she wouldn't trade her baby for the world.

When the front door slammed, Wren jumped.

"Hello?" Cash called.

"In here." With the backs of her hands she wiped still-damp cheeks.

Even barefoot, he towered over her. Despite the room's airy, open feel, the walls closed in around her. She'd never been the claustrophobic type, but his larger-than-life personality made it hard to breathe. Or maybe it was just those damned chaps!

A muscle ticking in his jaw, he turned his glare out the window. "I owe you an apology."

"Oh?"

"I should've handled this better. Truth is I'm kind of freaked out. This isn't the sort of thing that happens every day."

"Tell me about it." Even though Wren had had plenty of time to adjust, there were still days she couldn't get a grip on how far off course she'd strayed.

"When you get a chance," she said, "could you please get my rental agreement and overnight bag from my car? I'll call the agency for an extension."

"Will do. But let me give you a credit card to cover the extra days."

"Not necessary," she argued.

"How about you lie there making our baby and let me worry about everything else?"

"Seriously? You're able to say that with a straight face?" The sooner she got out of his home, the better. With that attitude, Cash Buckhorn sounded like a throwback to the days before Oklahoma had even been a state.

"What?" He blasted her with his smile. As usual, her traitorous body hummed under his spell. Just looking at him made her all hot and bothered. Luckily, there wouldn't be any additional touching between them. "You are making a baby, right?"

Having nothing more to say, she rolled over, blocking his powerful dimples from view.

"Not to change the subject," he said in a perfectly normal tone implying he still didn't *get* what he'd said to tick her off, "but I've got a big family. They're a bunch of busybodies. If you're going to be here a week, they're going to find out about it, and when they do, it's only fair I give you a heads-up."

"Regarding what?"

"The fact that you're carrying my child but don't have my ring on your finger."

"Isn't that archaic? The notion that a woman has to be married just to have a baby?"

He shrugged. "I couldn't agree more, but around here, folks see things differently."

"Is that what you want? To get married?"

"No offense, but no freaking way."

Though it was good news that his Old West chivalry ended at the very idea of a shotgun wedding, the vehemence behind his statement made her feel about as welcome as ants at a picnic. She'd always been so goal oriented that allowing a man into her life had never even been a priority. Sure, she'd let loose on a few weekends here and there, but for the most part, she stayed to herself, keeping her eyes on the prize of one day becoming a respected doctor. She dreamed of losing the stigma of having been a throwaway child. She wanted to feel needed and useful and above all, loved. "I appreciate your honesty. It's good we're both on the same page."

He actually sighed with relief. "So you don't think we should marry, either?"

"Of course not," she managed to say with a forced laugh. Although one day marriage was very much on her to-do list, for now it was out of the question.

Chapter Two

"You're pretty as the south pasture view." Georgina—Cash's mother and queen of the Buckhorn empire that included everything from cattle and quarter-horse breeding to oil—surveyed the mother of his child as if she were a filly up for auction. "A little on the scrawny side, but that's easily fixable with plenty of home cooking. Isn't that right, son?"

"Yes, ma'am," Cash muttered, wishing he hadn't told Dallas *everything* concerning Wren's visit. That way, he could've eased his mom into the matter. Kind of like you didn't want to jump into a cold pond on the first swim of summer, it wasn't a good idea letting your mom know you'd gotten a virtual stranger pregnant. If his mother found out, she'd have them to the courthouse within the hour. Which was why he was grateful to Wren for hiding her belly with an oversize purse. Cash had been all for keeping Wren's temporary presence on the ranch a secret, but she'd insisted on meeting his mother. Since in the twenty-four hours Wren had been in his home the color had returned to her cheeks, he'd agreed to a short outing before putting her back to bed.

"When Dallas told me his little brother had a woman

staying with him, I didn't believe it. Now that I've seen it with my own eyes, I need to know everything. How you met. Where you're from. Who your parents are. Don't skip a single detail."

Wren opened her mouth to speak, but thankfully Stella, nanny to Dallas's twin daughters, rounded the corner from the hall leading into the vaulted living room. The Western-themed grandeur of the ranch's main home made his look like a playhouse. "Whew. Betsy and Bonnie are at their friend Megan's. They're eating there, too, which means I'm free until at least eight." Only just noticing the stranger in the room, she said, "I'm sorry. I didn't know we had company."

"Stella Ward, meet Cash's new girl, Wren Barnes, from—I'm sorry. I never did hear where you're from." His five-ten mom wore her white hair in a low ponytail, and had tucked her blue plaid Western shirt into the waistband of her jeans. Out of her back pocket a pair of red leather gloves hung like a turkey wattle.

"Baltimore," Wren said.

"You're a long way from home," Stella noted. "How did you two meet?"

"At the Venetian in Vegas," Wren said.

"Yeah, we, um, fought over the same slot machine." Cash forced a grin. "She won."

Alongside Wren, he slipped his arm around her waist, begging her with a squeeze to keep her mouth shut about the reality of their situation.

Her pinched smile told him the jury was still out on her decision. Thank the Lord for that humongous purse!

"Must've been a good machine," his mother noted, lowering herself onto the custom sectional his dad had

had commissioned the year before he'd died. "I'm assuming this epic battle took place during your last rodeo out there?"

"Yes, ma'am." Cash further tightened his hold. "We've talked every night since. But then I got to thinking it was high time I saved myself some money by just flying the girl out here."

"But Henry told me there's a strange car parked at your house. Your daddy and I didn't raise you to make a guest travel all that way unaccompanied." Count on Henry not to keep his big mouth shut. The old guy had been working the ranch since Cash had been in diapers.

"It wasn't a big deal, Mrs. Buckhorn." She shifted her weight from one foot to the other, and it occurred to Cash that considering her condition, Wren might need to sit.

Come to think of it, the way his knee throbbed, copping a squat wasn't a half-bad idea.

Stella snorted. "Would be to me. Wren, I wouldn't have put up with that if I were you. Plus, I imagine that must've set you back a pretty penny."

"I'll pay her back," Cash said. "In not only money, but kisses." He smooched her cheek.

At which point she shoved him away. "Enough's enough. Mrs. Buckhorn, Stella, I'm sorry to have participated in this sham for even five minutes, but the truth of the matter is that…" Down went her purse, taking Cash's sinking stomach along with it. "I'm pregnant, and—"

"Oh, dear," said Georgina. "The way you carry on, Cash, I worried about something like this."

"Carry on? Before meeting Wren I'd been faithful to Ruby for two long weeks."

"That's my point. Two weeks? You're incapable of holding a meaningful relationship." She paced. "Your good looks were bound to get you in trouble. Even though you and Ruby had been on and off for years, she was all the time worrying about one of those buckle bunnies throwing themselves at you and one day coming away with the prize."

"Stop right there," Wren interjected. "I'm certainly not a buckle bunny, whatever that is, and Cash is hardly a prize, but my worst nightmare. For as long as I can remember, I've wanted a baby, but not like this. As we speak, I'm supposed to be deep into my first year of medical residency. Not stuck in Oklahoma with a no-good cowboy who doesn't even have the sense to buy a condom that won't break."

Georgina and Stella began talking at once.

Cash slipped his fingers into his mouth to whistle them quiet.

"First—" he directed his words to Wren "—it took two to tango, and honey, I don't recall hearing any complaints from you. Second," he said to his mother, "before you start nagging, I'm a full-grown man and don't need a lecture. Third—" he glared at his nieces' busybody nanny "—you stay out of this. It's none of your concern."

"It is," Stella countered, "if I have a wedding to put together in only a few days."

"Stop the bus," Cash said, holding up his hands. "No one said anything about a wedding. Wren and I agree the whole idea is archaic. Besides which, as long as her blood pressure checks out, she'll be gone within a week."

"If you were raised in a barn, getting married is archaic," his mother interjected.

Hands up, Wren said, "Please, the last thing I intended was to start all of this bickering."

"Yeah, well, you failed miserably." Cash shot her a glare before walking out the front door. "Couldn't you have held up the purse a few minutes longer?"

On her own with a pack of female wolves, Wren was unsure what to do with her hands. "You, ah, certainly have a lovely home, Mrs. Buckhorn."

"Thank you," Cash's mother said with a cold formality Wren didn't like nearly as well as her earlier, friendly way.

Clearing her throat, Georgina said, "I've never been one to beat around the bush, so here goes... While I certainly can't force you and my son to marry, the fact that you're carrying his child means a great deal to me." Crossing to an oak rolltop desk, she withdrew a checkbook and proceeded to write. "How much will it cost me to keep this baby in the family, starting by having it born with the Buckhorn name?"

"Y-you can't be serious," Wren said. "This isn't about money. At all. I wouldn't even be here if a freak fainting spell hadn't forced me to temporarily stay."

Stella asked, "Are you and the baby okay?"

"Fine," Wren assured her, "but my blood pressure was unusually high. Dr. Haven felt it was best that I stay off my feet this week—just to be safe. After that, I have to complete my residency as planned and Cash can, well..." She fidgeted with her hands. "Do whatever it is Cash does."

Sitting hard on the desk chair, Georgina Buckhorn didn't try hiding the fact that she'd started to cry—in the process making Wren feel all the worse for standing by her conviction to not only finish her education, but remain single while doing it.

"Georgia, hon," Stella soothed, up from the sofa and rubbing the older woman's back. "Everything's going to be okay."

"How?" Cash's mother wailed. "Both of them are clearly not in their right minds. In my day, when a woman got pregnant, she got married. There was none of this career mumbo jumbo."

"But you helped Duke with the ranch," Stella pointed out.

"That was different. This land was our mutual love," she said with a sniffle. Looking to her friend, she said, "Stella, would you mind fetching me a cool glass of sweet tea?"

The nanny scampered off.

"If you don't mind my asking—" Georgina shifted in her chair "—what do your folks think about all of this?"

"Honestly, ma'am..." Wren raised her chin. "I don't have *folks*. I've been on my own for as long as I can remember, which is why keeping this baby is so important." Cupping her hands to her belly, to the tiny life inside, she added, "More than anything, I want a family. Unfortunately, in order to properly care for my baby, I first need to finish my training. By no means is this the perfect scenario I've always dreamed of, but I'm a firm believer in playing the cards I've been dealt."

"WHO'S RUBY?"

Early evening, Cash looked up from shoveling manure to find the source of his consternation. Wren had changed from her uptight suit into a pair of jeans and a Johns Hopkins Med School T-shirt. Impressive. With a school pedigree like that, he could see why she wouldn't want to waste her life in Weed Gulch. "Shouldn't you be in bed?"

"Probably, but I'm going stir-crazy cooped up in the house."

Scowling, he asked, "What's wrong with my house?"

"Nothing," she assured him. "It's lovely. I'm just not used to having so much downtime."

"Oh." To avoid seeing the strain her nice, full breasts put on her shirt, Cash went back to shoveling. It was just his luck to not only be stuck with a pregnant hottie in the house for the next week, but not even be able to touch her. Maybe if he ignored her, she'd go away.

"You never answered my question. Ruby?"

No such luck. "Ruby was my somewhat recent past."

"Please stop being evasive and answer the question."

Leaning on his pitchfork, he wasn't sure where to begin.

"I gather you've known her awhile."

He grunted. "Like Mom said, on-and-off high school sweethearts—mostly *off*."

"If she meant so much, why haven't you married her?"

"Truth?" His facial features hardened. "Bull riding meant more. Which I guess gives us something in common, huh, Doc?"

Hefting herself onto a pile of hay bales, she made the universal sign of scales with her hands. "Riding bulls/saving lives. I fail to see the correlation."

"You wouldn't." Turning his back on her, he returned to work. His daddy had always said nothing cleared a cloudy mind like weary muscles. His aching knee knew the adage to be true.

"Whatever." After a deep sigh, she said, "Back to Ruby. If you wouldn't stop riding bulls long enough to marry her, why would your mother expect you to marry me? Makes no sense."

"Nope." Wishing she'd hush, Cash quickened his pace, hoping the harder he ignored her, the more she'd get the hint he wanted to be left alone.

"I mean, beyond sharing this baby, you and I have no connection. That means you're free to date, and one day marry, any woman you want."

"That simple, huh?" Judging by the furrow between her eyebrows, she wasn't quite as sold on the idea of him hooking up with another gal as she'd like him to believe. Good. If he was hurting from having to look at her gigantic pregnant boobs, he'd feel better knowing she wasn't happy, either.

Wren struggled for a coherent thought, eventually sputtering, "It could be—simple. If you'd let it." It wasn't fair that Cash had removed his shirt, turning her mind to mush. Having that bare chest pressed to hers had brought on the kind of heavy, sexual wanting she'd never dreamed possible. Which, in light of her current condition, was a fact she'd do well to remember.

This time around, he was strictly hands-off. Especially since with his golden curls kissed by honeyed evening sun, it was easy to imagine how beautiful their son or daughter would be.

"I've got work to do," he snapped.

"I only made an innocent comment. Why are you defensive?"

"You really wanna know?" Stabbing his pitchfork in hay, he raked his fingers through his hair. "Because aside from one insanely hot night, I don't even know you. Because what happened in my life before we met is none of your business. Because I just want a few minutes to myself to process the fact that like it or not I'm going to be a father. I've got a million reasons. Need more?"

Mutely, she shook her head.

He was right—on all counts. So why did that fact hurt? Why did she even care? In a week she and her baby would be on their way, and aside from what would hopefully be civilized holiday visits she'd rarely see him again.

"Damn, if I don't feel married already." After smacking the stable wall, he marched toward the house.

Upon noticing his backside was equally impressive, Wren felt her mouth go dry. If only she didn't have those wild Vegas flashbacks to contend with. Maybe then she'd stand a fighting chance at keeping her mind on task. As for where her body was headed...

The baby she carried pretty much said it all!

THIRTY MINUTES LATER Cash pushed himself out of the pool and grabbed for a towel. A swim always cleared the fog from his brain. Too bad his knee still hurt like hell.

The morning's rain was long gone and with sun beating on wet prairie, the day had been a scorcher. The scent of drying chlorine already rose from the pavement.

He reluctantly headed for the house. Wren carried his child. Shouldn't he at least feel warm and fuzzy toward her? Instead, the notion of not only seeing her again, but being stuck with her for a week was incomprehensible.

What would they talk about? Would his mother keep riding him about marrying? Couldn't she just accept the fact that he had reasons he wasn't ready to head down the aisle—damned good ones?

He found Wren in his guest room, lying crossways on the bed reading, damn near camouflaged by clothes. T-shirts, shorts and silky, lacy unmentionables, the mere sight of which had him shifting his fly to a more comfortable position. Their night in Vegas hadn't been merely hot, but more like an inferno. Where was *that* woman now? And how the hell had she squeezed so much into an overnight bag?

"You okay?" he asked.

"Sure." After raising her gaze from the pages of what looked to be a steamy, pirate-ravishing-a-maiden saga, she rolled onto her side. "Why?"

"You look like an old cat I used to have. She'd spend hours ripping up my room, then lounge among the wreckage, purring like a feline queen."

Wren laughed. "No purring for me. Just exhaustion. I got off to a great start unpacking, but I seem to have a tenth of my normal energy. It's a drag."

"Sorry." Not sure what to do with his hands, he settled on crossing his arms.

"What're you apologizing for?"

"Not to brag, but it was my superhuman seed that got you into this predicament." After capping off his outrageous statement with the slow grin that universally got him out of hot water with women of all ages, he yanked off his towel, using it to wipe down his still-water-beaded chest.

Wren rolled her eyes. "Never have I encountered an ego bigger than yours."

"Thanks." He rubbed his damp hair. "I think." He'd just started unfastening his swim trunk's button-fly when the good almost-doctor cleared her throat.

"Do you mind?" Slapping down her book, she raised her eyebrows a good inch.

"Mind what?"

"Not undressing in front of me."

"In case you've forgotten, we might be strangers when it comes to knowing each other's favorite colors and foods. But in the biblical sense, back in Vegas, we pretty much become experts on each other's anatomy. Think it's a little late for you to now turn shy."

It didn't take special psychological training to see that she struggled keeping her eyes off him.

"It's all right, you know." He gave his chest and abs a flourish. "You're allowed to look."

Not only did she grab for the nearest eye covering, but she said, "For the duration of my stay, it would be most appreciated if you'd disrobe in your own room."

On that, he had to laugh. Two could play this game. "Oh, honey, I'll keep my naked body behind closed doors as long as you quit waving those she-devil scraps you call panties in front of your face."

Yanking them down to see that she had indeed covered her eyes with lace, she growled.

He smiled and took his sweet time sauntering all the way into *his* shower.

Chapter Three

"Could you please speed it up?"

Standing in front of a pen filled with adorably chirping, fuzzy yellow chicks, Wren shot Cash a dirty look. They'd shared a house for all of two days and already the man drove her nuts. "Since I'm still dizzy, I told you I could ask your mother to drive me to town for shampoo. Then I wouldn't have had you nagging me over every little thing."

"And I told you, nobody carts around my pregnant woman but me. You're my responsibility. Besides, even if Mom had driven you, I was already headed to the feed store, so what was the point in wasting two tanks of gas?" In honor of their being out in civilization—if Weed Gulch and all ten of its downtown stores could even be considered civilized—Cash had at least worn clean boots and a long-sleeved baby-blue shirt that did wicked-good things to his green eyes. Not to be too formal, he'd left his shirttails loose. His straw cowboy hat looked as if it had been sat on one too many times and then run over by a tractor. Despite that fact, even at the feed store Cash drew women the way cupcakes drew kindergartners.

"Afternoon, Miss Lucy." He tipped his hat to a pigtailed five-year-old who was kicking the fool out of a gumball machine. "What seems to be the problem?"

"It took my money."

Kneeling, he plucked her fallen quarter from the concrete floor. "Wouldn't happen to be this money, would it?"

Arms around him for a hug, she said, "Thanks, Cash."

"You're most welcome."

Moving a few aisles farther, he asked Wren, "Want me to buy you some chicks?"

"What would I do with them?"

He shot her an indecipherable look before moving deeper into the store. His long-legged stride made it impossible for her to keep up, so she didn't even try, instead losing herself in the novelty of a place that sold not only live chickens but veterinary supplies, denim overalls and Crock-Pots. The rich scent of grain mingled with that of freshly popped popcorn—given away free with every purchased can of coconut popping oil.

Mouth watering, she grabbed a still-warm bag as well as everything needed to make the snack at home.

"Cash Buckhorn," said a big-haired blonde near a cardboard weed-killer display, "as I live and breathe. Been doing much dating since that knee has you stuck in town?"

"Nope." He took two pairs of leather gloves from a rack. One pair large. The other small. "Heard you stood up for Ruby at her wedding."

Eyes closed, the woman hugged herself, expression dreamy. "It was the most gorgeous ceremony ever. You know how Ruby's daddy prides himself on having the prettiest barn in three counties? Well, he had it decked out so fancy you'd be hard-pressed to even tell horses usually live there."

"That's nice." A muscle ticked in Cash's jaw.

"Ruby thought it might've been awkward had she sent you an invitation."

He shrugged. "She'd have been right."

Careful to remain in the shadows of rakes and hoes, Wren continued peeking around the wood handles, curious as to where this conversation was leading.

"You poor thing." Hands on her hips, the mystery woman cocked her head. "You're as heartsick as a kitten leaving its litter. Come to the Grange Hall dance with me Saturday night. It'll be just what you need."

"Love to," he said, "but besides my bum knee, I can't."

"Oh?"

"Yes, ma'am." He sidestepped the woman to snag a gaping Wren around her waist. "Please meet the mother of my child, Dr. Wren Barnes. Since she'll be bunking with me till week's end, even if my knee worked, it'd hardly be proper for me to go dancing with you."

Before Wren could answer, Cash planted on her lips a kiss so hot that she thought if he kept it up much longer, her popcorn-making supplies would burst without a stove!

"WHY'D YOU DO THAT?" Wren demanded once Cash had her back in his truck.

"You being a city gal," he said with a sideways glance while backing out of the lot, "and looking about twenty months pregnant, you wouldn't understand."

"Try me." As amazing as the kiss had been for a

feverish few seconds, the aftermath had been a nightmare. She'd always been a private person, and it had never occurred to her that it was even possible to know every single person in a store. But Cash did. And now all those people were under the impression that she was Cash's *girl*. Only, she wasn't. Fortunately, she'd soon be gone, leaving him on his own to chase the tails of whatever lies he'd spun.

Since her companion obviously had no logical explanation for his unappreciated—although decidedly expert—advances, Wren focused on the scenery. Weed Gulch boasted one main road, which also happened to be a state highway. On that road there were two stoplights. One at the intersection in front of the town hall. The other at the entrance to the local school that housed kindergarten through grade twelve, all on the same campus. According to the Kiwanis Club sign, the Weed Gulch Wagoneers had been 1A state baseball champs in 1989.

Here and there were housing subdivisions mixed in with mobile homes and barns. Reasor's Grocery stood adjacent to a pasture filled with grazing cattle. A fieldstone library was squeezed between a mom-and-pop barbecue restaurant and the shell of an old convenience store that now served as a used car lot.

"You may not understand that kiss," Cash said out of the blue, "but trust me, sometimes these things have to get done." Veering onto the county road leading to the dirt road that led to the ranch, Cash said, "Ruby used to be mine. Now, all because I didn't feel the timing was right for me to settle down, she's already gotten herself married to another guy. Tell me, does that sound right?"

Wren angled to face him. "In other words, in a perfect world she should have spent her whole life waiting for you to be ready?"

"I never said anything of the sort."

"Uh-huh." Frowning, she added, "Which leads us right back to my question of if you didn't want to marry her, why do you even care that some other guy did?"

"I don't. Not really." One hand on the wheel, with his other he fished a stick of Big Red from the pack he kept on the dash. Her mouth watered from the sweet cinnamon smell, but she refused to give him the pleasure of asking for a piece. "Truth is we'd long ago grown apart. The twentieth time around with her only told me what I already knew—together we had smokin' chemistry, but little else." Thoughtfully chewing, he added, "This is more of an ego thing. I'm easily the best-looking man in the county. Can't have people thinking I'm not worthy of marriage."

"Your head gets any bigger, you'll have to add a sunroof for you to fit in your own truck."

He winked, leading her to the conclusion that her dig hadn't bothered him in the least. What did was the notion of him being with this Ruby in an intimate manner. Why, she couldn't say, but with his baby growing inside her, she couldn't bear to think of his skilled hands being on any other woman's curves.

"What's wrong with your knee?" she asked, to clear her mind of irrational jealousy.

"Nothing."

She pressed, "Then why do you sometimes walk with

a limp and you told the blonde back at the feed store that your knee's *bum?*"

"Long story," he said with a glance out his window. He didn't say another word, and his clenched jaw and tightened hold on the wheel told her to stay out of his business.

A GOOD FIFTEEN MILES down the road, Cash slowed upon finding Doc Haven's white cargo van pulled in front of Delores Hawke's place.

Slamming on the brakes to avoid hitting the town doctor who'd run into the middle of the road, Cash instinctively stretched out his arm to brace Wren. "Hold on...."

The white-haired doctor jogged to Cash's side of the truck.

Cash lowered his window. "Need help?"

"And then some," the older man said, struggling to catch his breath. "Delores took a tumble from her kitchen stool. Not only broke her hip, but put a nasty gash on her head. County ambulance is clear over in Marquette dealing with a cardiac arrest. Can you help me get her stabilized and in the back of my van?"

"Absolutely," Cash said, already pulling to the side of the road.

The elderly woman's home was stifling, reeking of Bengay and mothballs, and at least ten degrees warmer than the muggy eighty outside. Sidestepping stacked newspapers and yarn-filled baskets, they finally reached the moaning woman.

Kneeling alongside Delores, oblivious to the blood, Wren took the woman's hand, smoothing the top, assuring her everything would be okay.

Wren helped herself to alcohol swabs from the doctor's bag and cleaned Delores's forehead. Though the wound had bled a lot, it looked to be superficial. Cash had been hurt enough during his rodeo days that he knew the difference between a major blow and one that'd let you finish out your rides.

Wren distracted the older woman further by making small talk and then holding firmly to her hand while Cash and Doc hefted her onto a gurney.

Within minutes, the pain meds Doc had loaded into Delores's IV conked her right out.

"Whew," Doc said once they'd gotten the patient settled in the back of the air-conditioned van. Removing his cowboy hat, he used his shirtsleeve to wipe sweat from his brow. "I sure am glad you two came along when you did."

"Why didn't you call the house?" Cash asked.

"I did. Only, no one picked up." Looking to Wren, the man said, "I appreciate the help, but why are you out of bed?"

Wren looked sheepish. "We just made a quick run to the store."

"Hmmph." Doc Haven frowned. "Well, try to take it easy from here on." He paused, then added, "You certainly have a way with patients and seem familiar with a head wound. Nurse?"

"She's nearly a doctor," Cash offered, unexpectedly proud of Wren's achievements. "Graduated from Johns Hopkins."

Doc whistled. "Dang, girl. With a fancy pedigree like that, you probably already know more than me."

"I would hardly say that." Wren reddened. Her flushed cheeks made her look younger. Less world-weary than her usual concentrated expression. Patting her belly, she said, "I'm supposed to be in my residency now, but life sort of got in the way."

Eyeing Cash and then her, he harrumphed. "In my day, folks got married before having babies."

Cash grinned. "Back in your day, you also didn't have microwave ovens or HDTV."

"Your point being?" The doctor put his bag on the truck's passenger side.

"Only that whether we're married or not doesn't make a hill-of-beans difference to this little guy or gal." He cinched his arm around Wren's waist. He couldn't pinpoint why, but it made him inordinately glad that she was as forward thinking in her anti-marriage views as he was.

"YOU'VE HARDLY SAID A WORD since we've been home." Cash finished unloading the feed from the truck to find Wren at the kitchen table, a cookie in one hand and her pirate book in the other.

"You're still not talking to me?" Easing onto a counter stool, he noted, "And seeing how much you like hearing your own voice, I must've done something pretty bad."

She treated him with a glare.

"At least you're looking at me. Somewhat of an improvement." He pitched a wadded napkin at her.

"Stop," she barked. "I'm at a good part and would appreciate not being disturbed."

"I'm sorry, okay? Whatever I did this time for you to be mad at me, I'm a miserable excuse of a human, lower than the manure lining the soles of my work boots." Off the stool, he was suddenly behind her, folding his arms around her, squeezing her tight.

Breaking free, she fairly flew to the side of the cramped room that he wasn't on. "Lay off the charm. I'm immune."

"You wish." He winked, and as if on cue, the butterflies in her traitorous tummy fluttered. "Come on," he coaxed, moving close to her. "You know you wanna tell me why I'm the most wretched beast to ever roam the earth."

Tired of fighting, Wren allowed herself a few minutes' surrender. Leaning against him, soaking in his strength was akin to removing twin bricks from her shoulders. "It's stupid."

"The reason you're upset?"

She nodded. He'd wrapped her in a backward bear hug and she circled his muscular forearms with her hands, resting her cheek on his shoulder. His T-shirt smelled clean and fresh, his skin like baked-in sun and soap and that unique something she inherently knew was him. Like it or not, a part of him grew inside her.

"Out with it," he urged.

"All day you've told anyone who would listen that I'm carrying your baby. When the doctor asked if we were tying the knot, you seemed to delight in telling him we aren't."

Tensing against her, he noted, "I don't *delight*—ever."

"Whatever you want to call it, I got the notion you were sticking it to everyone who's ever told you what to do. Using our baby to thumb your nose at their conventionalism."

He took a long time to answer. "That's not true.

I'm just relieved you feel the same way about getting hitched. I'm not ready for that, and to be honest, I'm not sure I ever will be."

Fighting the knot in her throat, Wren said, "Fair enough. But if you're so relieved to be free of a binding relationship, then why did you kiss me? Why are you holding me?"

Slowly, softly he spun her to face him. "Beyond the baby, the night you and I shared was hands down the hottest of my life."

Heat roared through her, flustering her mind to the point that it was impossible to think.

His touch was tender, radiating warmth as he brushed her throat with his thumbs. "Dare you to tell me you haven't replayed it a hundred times."

She wanted him so badly to kiss her that her lips actually hurt. "I—I'm also mad at you for not trusting me enough to tell me what's wrong with your knee."

"It's nothing to get worked up about. You and me, however..." He sharply exhaled. "Remember how we started out fast, but ended up slow? Which time do you think it was?"

Sliding his big hands along her silhouette, past the sides of her aching breasts, in at her waist, out at her hips, he knelt before her, lifting the hem of her T-shirt, pressing his open mouth against her womb.

Between her legs a low hum both dizzied and thrilled. Hands in his hair, steadying herself against his advances, she felt her breathing turn shallow. Her pulse became frenzied.

"You know, like how did we make our baby? On the lanai lounge chairs? Standing with your back pressed against the sliding glass door? In that big, soft bed with you riding me until—"

"Stop," she begged. Her voice was unrecognizable. Thick with ghost passion from a night she'd tried to forget. "It doesn't matter how our baby was made, only that he or she has become our future. Trouble is, I already have one—in Baltimore. I have to focus on that." *I can't afford to lose myself in you.*

"Once the baby is born, you don't want any contact with me?"

"In a perfect world, that'd be great." Ducking her head, she escaped to the fridge for a refill on her decaffeinated iced tea. "That said, it's not my intention to keep you from your child."

Jaw hard, he nodded and stood.

"It's entirely up to you how much contact you want." The tea was refreshing. Cash's cold stare? Not so much.

"But if I want that connection with my son or daughter, I'll have to go out East to get it?"

Chapter Four

"Sorry about not having the latest on-site ultrasound," Doc Haven said Friday during Wren's thirty-week pregnancy exam. Assuming everything went well, he'd clear her for travel. He bustled about the room that was decorated in a Sesame Street theme. "Tulsa has everything a body could ever need in regard to medical gadgets. If I run into something I can't handle I send folks to one of my associates over there. Speaking of which, remember our patient with the broken hip?"

"Cash's neighbor, Delores?"

"That's the one. Her surgery was a success and she's convalescing nicely at a short-term care center. Thanks again for your help."

"All I did was hold her hand."

"Sometimes that's what's most needed."

A freckle-faced redhead sporting a high ponytail and pink scrubs took Wren's blood pressure. "One forty-eight over ninety-two."

"Smidge higher than I'd like. Anyway, I'll give Cash Delores's address. If you happen to be that way, you might stop by. I'm sure she'd love the company." Taking a fetal Doppler monitor from a countertop charging station, he squeezed a dollop of ultrasound gel on her belly, and then applied gentle pressure until he found her baby's heartbeat. "He's a strong little fella."

"I think it's a girl," Wren said. Hearing her future child's galloping pulse never failed to thrill. She'd invited Cash to sit in on this portion of her exam, but he'd declined. Probably just as well. The more attached he grew to their child, the harder it would be for him to let him or her go.

"You don't want to find out for sure?"

Wren shook her head. "I've always liked surprises."

"Me, too," he admitted while checking her wrists, hands and ankles for fluid retention. "I miss that part of birthing babies. If God had meant us to know every little thing about these tykes, he would've installed a peephole."

Wren laughed.

Her ultimate dream—although, with the baby, it might now be out of reach—was to become a heart surgeon just like her idol and friend Dr. Abigail West, but she could see where being a country doctor would have its upside. On a good day Doc Haven covered every specialty from obstetrics to geriatrics. She supposed a country practice would be satisfying, but in a different way. Not the kind of rush stemming from a successful open-heart surgery, but more of a quiet satisfaction grounded in knowing his patients for a lifetime.

The baby's position was charted and then a lab technician popped in to tell the doctor that her urine sample checked normal for sugar, but high for protein.

"Thanks for working me in," Wren said once her examination was complete.

"My pleasure. I'm proud to say I delivered all three Buckhorn boys and the lone girl."

"Cash has a sister?"

Snapping off his gloves, the doctor nodded. "Took off a while back. No one's sure where. Georgina misses her something fierce. It's a mystery to me why she even left. Oklahoma has everything a soul could ever need."

Wren wasn't so sure. "What's your verdict? Am I free to make immediate flight plans?"

He shook his head. "Before your appointment I had a conference call with your big-city ob-gyn, Dr. Patten, and she agreed that if your blood pressure and urine protein were still up, we feel it's best you stay calm and relaxed. As much as you can, it also wouldn't hurt you to stay off your feet."

"But that's ridiculous. I have to get back to my residency. I owe my roommates rent money and have other obligations I can't just abandon."

Sighing, the older man crossed his arms. "Let me put it this way. Right now we're concerned. Plainly, your body was telling you that in your current condition, travel is a major stressor. You've been at rest for a week, and your levels are still not anywhere near normal. I'm not ready to diagnose preeclampsia yet, but you're close. Unless you want to be an ideal candidate for stroke, heart disease, kidney failure, delivering your baby premature or God forbid, even stillborn, you need to heed this as a warning. Slow down and let that man out in the waiting room take care of you."

Refusing to let the doctor's words take root, Wren asked, "What does that mean for my residency? I'll be back in another week or so?"

"Considering the fact that you had high blood pressure before you even got here, added to your now high protein levels and recent fainting spell, it is my and Dr. Patten's professional opinion that you remain on bed rest for the remainder of your pregnancy."

"That's ridiculous," Wren snapped. "I can't just—"

"Whoa. Cool that temper of yours right on down, little lady." Reaching for the blood pressure cuff attached to the wall, he took a reading. "One fifty-five over ninety-four."

"Are you sure?"

His stern expression told her that not only was he insulted by her second-guessing his reading, but fed up with her arguments.

Preeclampsia was nothing to fool around with. Bottom line, no matter how badly she wanted to get back to work, she wanted a healthy baby more.

Ten minutes later she returned to the waiting area to find Cash asleep in a chair, long legs sprawling in front of him, his straw hat covering his eyes. His light snoring didn't bother an elderly woman's knitting or a mother settling a fight between her two little kids.

"Cash?" Hand on his shoulder, she gave him a gentle shake.

He jolted awake. "Time for the baby?"

She squatted to pick up his hat from the floor. "Still ten to twelve weeks."

"Oh." Rubbing his eyes with the heels of his hands, he said, "I was just dreaming that I was at a rodeo when you went into labor."

"I suppose that could happen." After handing him his hat, resigned to the fact that she wasn't going anywhere soon, she made her way to the check-out clerk to schedule her next appointment. "Are you entered in one around then?"

"You ask too many questions. And wait a minute..." Just outside the office he stopped and eyed her. "Why'd you make an appointment with Doc Haven? Thought you were going home?"

"Surprise," she said with deadpan enthusiasm. "My blood pressure's still sky-high and I've been ordered to stay off my feet for the duration."

"Yeah, but what's that mean?" Even confused, he was much too handsome. How was she ever going to manage living with him until her baby's anticipated Christmas delivery?

"Basically that through no decision of our own, we've become roomies for the duration of my pregnancy— barring an unlikely blood pressure miracle."

"So you're still sick?"

She nodded and headed toward the truck. But he wasn't finished questioning and he snagged her wrist.

"But as long as you don't overdo it, you and the baby are going to be fine?"

"Yes," she said, hating the pleasant tingles he caused with his slightest touch. Her whole life, she'd been in control. Now not only didn't she decide where she lived or who she lived with, but her body betrayed her, too, whenever Cash was around.

"It won't be that bad."

"You're not upset?" Because she certainly was.

"About you staying on?" He grinned. "Might be fun. The doc didn't say anything about you restricting certain athletic bedroom activities, did he?"

She wrenched her arm free to give Cash a swat.

The day was clear and warm with the winds at peace.

Why couldn't she shake the feeling that until she escaped Oklahoma, she might never feel that way? Should she take a chance with her and their baby's health? Betting that her blood pressure wouldn't become too great a problem if she flew home?

Still grinning, Cash used a remote to unlock his black truck. The doors had Buckhorn Ranch arched across them, with battling rams beneath.

Upon opening her side, he offered his hand. "Yep, this could definitely work to my advantage. We could exchange sex for butler service. Kinky good fun, huh?" That white-toothed smile of his flipped her stomach. She would've liked to blame it on the baby, but considering the heat between them every time they touched, no one but Cash could be to blame.

"You're horrible! I would never have sex with you."

Clearing his throat, Cash reminded her with a laugh, "Hate to be the bearer of bad news, but judging by the size of my bun in your oven, you kind of already did."

Ignoring him, she rolled her eyes.

He circled to his side of the truck, climbed in and started the engine.

"Back to a more polite conversational topic, you never answered my rodeo question. Will you be around during the holidays?" Hoping to counteract the stifling heat, Wren turned on the AC.

"Officially, yes, I am supposed to be riding in a holiday rodeo, but because of my knee, I'm suspended from the pro tour. Happy?"

"No." She adjusted the vents to blow gale-force cooling wind on her face. "That's the last thing I want."

"Then why even bring it up?"

"I was curious. That's all. No hidden agenda."

Maneuvering Weed Gulch's main drag with its assortment of pickups, slow-moving blue-haired women in Caddies on their way to Alma's Kut & Kurl and too many harried moms in minivans, Cash hardened his jaw.

What was he thinking? During their time together, would she ever learn to decipher his multitude of expressions? Considering the fleeting nature of their relationship, would she even want to? The whole point of her staying was about maintaining or improving her current level of health while bringing an equally healthy baby into the world. Nothing about that plan involved becoming fast friends with her baby's father.

"Hungry?" Cash asked.

"Always. What'd you have in mind?"

"Queenie's twisty cones are always good on a warm day. Want one?"

"Will they dip it in that chocolate stuff that hardens into a shell?"

Glancing her way, he grinned. "You like your ice cream that way, too?"

Disregarding the pleasant tingle that was becoming a habit every time Cash smiled, she said, "Doesn't everyone?"

SHARING A PICNIC TABLE in the dappled shade of a pecan tree, Cash reckoned he got more pleasure from watching Wren devour her cone than he did eating his own.

She had this sexy-sweet habit of licking the base that was causing a tremendous amount of below-the-belt discomfort. Trying to get his mind out of the bedroom, he noted, "All kidding aside, hope you're not too upset about not getting to go home. Promise, I'll try making your stay as stress free as possible."

"Thanks." Lick, lick.

Cash shifted his fly.

"I never realized how much stress affects me. It's scary."

"I'm sure." Reaching for her free hand, he gave her a squeeze. "Now that we're a team, though, it's okay to chill. At least let me shoulder some of the emotional burden you've been carrying." It had to have been tough—not only finding out she was pregnant on her own, but then having difficulties. Just thinking about it got him all choked up. What if something bad happened to her or the baby? "Sorry."

"For what?" She'd finished her cone and now wiped her fingers with a napkin. His mind's eye saw her one day down the road, fastidiously helping their little boy or girl clean after a sticky treat.

"Going through the majority of your pregnancy alone. I should've been there."

"Stop. My purpose in being here isn't to ply you with guilt. I'm entirely to blame for not telling you sooner." Head bowed, she haltingly admitted, "For not admitting to myself that I needed help sooner. Guess now my body's making the call for me."

Leaning forward, elbows on the sun-warmed wooden table, he asked, "Why were you reluctant to come to me? Did you think I wouldn't care?"

Swallowing hard, she focused on the family foursome next in line for ice cream. "You have to understand that my whole life, I've been on my own. To even acknowledge I need help is a big step. Huge."

"What do you mean you've always been on your own?"

Meeting his gaze, she said, "My earliest memories are of a church-run orphanage. While I was more than adequately fed, clothed and educated, when it came to affection, there was precious little to go around—especially once I grew older." Shrugging, she wiped tears from her eyes when she thought he wasn't looking. "After a while I figured I was better off without any touchy-feely stuff. When it came to my studies, I compensated for a lack of outside attention by overachieving. Inside, I wasn't happy with anything less than the best. Up until now, that ideal has served me well."

"But to a certain extent—I mean, aside from your deciding to sleep with me—neither pregnancy nor your residency being interrupted was in any way under your control."

After a faint laugh, she wadded her napkin into a tight ball. "No kidding."

Save for the air conditioner's steady humming, the ride home was mostly silent. Cash's mind wandered to images of Wren as a small girl, sitting alone in the corner of some institutional playroom with few toys and even fewer friends. Though he knew it was the last thing she'd have wanted, his heart went out to the lonesome little girl. He had the craziest urge to shower her with pretty, girlie things and ensure she always had a surplus of hugs.

Growing up, he'd been blessed with an overabundance of not only material things, but parental attention. His dad was a local legend. Famed for being a shrewd oilman and cattleman. Always fair, yet firm. His dad had been as manly as they come, but not so much that he ever shied from giving his boys plenty of pats on their backs and all-around affection. Duke Buckhorn had been such a remarkable parent and husband that often Cash felt lost in his shadow.

When he rode and crowds cheered, he temporarily escaped. Now, with his messed-up knee, even that respite was at risk.

Truth be told, that was why he never wanted to marry or spend his life working this family ranch. How would he ever live up to his father's monumental ghost?

"DR. WEST?" Once home, after calling the rental car agency and arranging to drop it off, Wren stood in Cash's den, hoping she stayed strong through the duration of this second call.

"Well," Wren's idol said in a friendly tone, "if it isn't my favorite resident. Are you back at the hospital?"

"N-not exactly." She explained her situation. "With all of that in mind, I'm temporarily stuck—but excited about getting back to work as soon as I'm physically able."

"Of course, I understand." The petite powerhouse, who wore a no-nonsense bob that always managed to look impeccable, sighed. Never a good sign. "That said, I can't help but find myself wishing this baby had never happened. I'm happy for you, but sad at the same time."

"I understand." Wren could feel Dr. West's disappointment in her.

"I've lost a lot of promising candidates due to so-called love, and I refuse to lose you, Wren Barnes. As long as we're on the same page about that, I'll move heaven and earth to get you back into the program."

"Thank you." Wren's whole body quivered with relief. Up until now, she hadn't realized just how afraid she'd been of potentially being booted from her chosen resident program, but with Dr. West on her side, she had nothing to fear.

THAT NIGHT, WATCHING the sunset from the back-porch swing, Cash sipped from a longneck beer. The scent of barbecued chicken on the grill made his stomach rumble. Damned if the day hadn't been so messed up he'd forgotten to eat. "Is it just me, or is this whole setup a little..."

"Awkward?" The soon-to-be mother of his child flashed a faint smile.

"I was going to say surreal, but your word works, too." Since they shared the porch's only seat, necessity forced his thigh against hers. He wore jeans and a T-shirt. She'd changed into khaki shorts and a pink maternity tank that managed to all at once be sexy and demure. Their shoulders brushed as they shifted position. The sensation was electrifying—and all too reminiscent of the night that had brought them to their current predicament.

He cleared his throat and stood.

"Hard as I try," he said, "I can't wrap my head around what's happened. You showing up at my place. Pregnant." Worse yet, his body hadn't gotten the memo that he wasn't supposed to still be attracted to her. "Now sick and forced to stay."

"I know."

Ambling off the porch, trying to hide his limp, he took another drag from his beer before turning the chicken and brushing on more of his famous sweet sauce he usually reserved for special occasions.

Edging sideways, she raised her feet onto the swing, hugging her knees. "For what it's worth, I am sorry about you missing your holiday rodeo—and any others, too. If you have a miraculous recovery, please feel free to leave me in the housekeeper's care. That way, once I have the baby, I can head home and for you, it'll be like I've never been here."

"Way to make a man feel needed." He lowered the lid on the grill.

"Of course you are."

Shaking his head, he laughed. "You're some piece of work."

"What's that supposed to mean?"

The fact that she saw no potential problem with her plan to take their baby off to Baltimore and rarely see him again irked Cash to no end. Even better, it put his attraction for Wren into perspective. What he felt for her was physical—nothing more. "The chicken will be ready in about twenty minutes. I'm going to make a salad."

"Need help?"

"No, thanks."

"Cash…" She rose, hugging herself as if she were chilled. "When I decided to try finding you, I'd hoped we could be friends. This afternoon, over ice cream, I thought we'd made giant strides toward that end. Now I'm getting the sense that we're right back where we started."

Why, he couldn't say, but her statement struck him as asinine.

Turning his back on her, he went inside. He had

developed a major soft spot for Wren, but then she'd reminded him that her real name was Miss Independence. She didn't need him, or anyone else for that matter. If it hadn't been for her high blood pressure, she'd have long since put her sweet behind on an eastbound plane.

Unfortunately, she followed. "Think about it. Like it or not, we'll now be sharing birthdays and holidays and milestones like first words and steps and graduations. Do you really want to spend all of those precious moments wearing a scowl?"

What he wanted was never to have been put in this situation, but that was a moot point. He couldn't put his finger on why, but he was suddenly mad as hell at the woman. Not about the baby. He'd been the one who'd purchased a faulty condom. But dammit, he'd lived twenty-seven years as a carefree bachelor and he wasn't even ready to have kids, let alone a ready-made, move-in wife.

Rummaging in the fridge for the prepackaged Caesar salad they'd picked up at the store, he found it, then conked his head on the top shelf as he straightened. "Damn!"

"You all right?" Her voice brimmed with soft concern. As if she genuinely cared about his well-being. At his side, she fished her fingers through his hair. "Let me have a look."

"I'm fine," he said, drawing away. It further irked him that she was being nice while he struggled for baseline civility. "Just hurts like a son of a—well, you know."

She closed the refrigerator door. "Since you don't need help with your head, want me to make the salad?"

"You're pregnant."

"And?" Leaning against the counter's edge, she folded her arms.

"You should be sitting." He took a glass bowl from the cabinet alongside the stove. "Doing a good job of growing my baby."

After a long pause and expression hot enough to start a barn fire, she got all up in his face. "Look here, Cash Buckhorn, I've had just about all I care to take of you blowing hot and then cold and your asinine, archaic pregnancy observations. Either you straighten up or I'm figuring out a way to safely hightail it back to Baltimore. It might be rough going, but nothing could be as bad as living with you like this."

Chapter Five

"Truce?" Wren glanced up from the book she was reading to see Cash at her bedroom door, waving a few sheets of toilet paper. He looked so ridiculous, she didn't have the heart to stay mad, especially since she'd skipped Cash's barbecued chicken and she was now starving. "We happen to be fresh out of white flags."

"Okay, truce," she said, resting her novel on her lap.

When he entered the room, all the oxygen left. The night was warm, with crickets singing outside open windows. Cash wore no shirt and his blond curls were a rummaged-through mess. His sleepy-sexy grin made it impossible for her to stay mad.

Perched on the foot of the bed, he said, "Sorry for earlier. Not sure what got into me."

"Probably the same initial rush of frustration and apprehension and excitement I've already been through." Smiling, she added, "You forget, I've already had a while to accept the inevitable."

"So? How did you work it out?" Looking away and then back, he admitted, "Straight up, I'm angry with you, but I don't know why."

"Do you resent me showing up on your doorstep,

pretty much taking over your life?" Adjusting the pillows behind her, she leaned forward.

"Oddly enough, no. I don't think that's it."

"Then why?" With their new forced proximity, she needed to know what was broken between them in order to fix it. But then, seeing as how there was no "them" outside one wild night, maybe that was the problem.

"I'm miffed you waited six months to tell me I'm going to be a father. What? Was I so horrible to be with you couldn't bear to see me again?"

Tears stung her eyes. "I already told you, I prefer handling things on my own."

"Our baby isn't an item on your to-do list."

"I never said it was."

Shaking his head as though he was exasperated, he turned to leave.

Wren called out, "Please, stay."

He stopped, but didn't face her. "Why?"

"Because I'm sorry I didn't tell you sooner. I should have. But regardless, you deserved to be along for the *ride,* start to finish." She grinned.

"And I'm damned good-looking." He turned and sat next to her on the bed, every spellbinding, muscular ripple on his chest entirely too close for comfort.

"Wh-what?"

"Admit it."

"I will not." Even if it was true.

"You owe me that much."

"Why? Are we back to your bruised ego again? Because if you're worried about something ridiculous like I didn't find you attractive enough to be in my life, then you're certifiable."

"But in a hunky sort of way, right?"

His expression suddenly held such genuine concern, she couldn't help but laugh.

"This isn't funny."

"It is to me," she said with another giggle. "How are you going to be a father when the only thing you care about is the continued worship of you?"

"That's not true. Is it so wrong to want a little validation?"

No. It was something she'd secretly yearned for her entire life. "Okay, for what it's worth, you are easily the most heartbreakingly handsome cowboy stud I've ever seen. If you hadn't been, I never would've slept with you."

"Thank you." He winked. "It's about time you admitted it."

"Beast!" she cried, giving that gorgeous chest of his a swat. "Are you ever going to feed me? Or are you just going to stand there admiring yourself?"

"THIS IS THE ONE PLACE in town I've never been." When Cash had agreed to take Wren to the library, he hadn't planned on going inside, but now that he had, he found it wasn't half-bad. Bond money had newly remodeled the space to be light and airy with skylights and plenty of picture windows overlooking the town duck pond. Potted plants filled every corner and the children's area with its thick blue carpet, yellow furniture and green-eggs-and-ham wall mural looked straight from the pages of Dr. Seuss.

"You're kidding?" Wren said, heading straight for a spinning rack loaded with more of her pirate books.

"Nope. In fact, I've made it a mission to stay away.

Many women have tried coercing me in here, but all until you have failed."

Hands on what was left of her hips, she cocked her head, spilling her cute ponytail over her right shoulder. Her gray eyes were bright, her complexion glowing— he'd have been hard-pressed to find a more attractive woman. Not that he'd ever tell her. The house wasn't big enough to hold both their egos should she realize her own level of attractiveness. "You are so making that up."

"You got me." He cracked a smile. "But if you hurry, we'll have time for the lunch special at Ron's."

"What's that?"

"Best hamburger in the state. It's out by the toll road, but well worth the drive."

Glancing at the cover of a book and then the back, she said, "I'm still full from breakfast."

"Then as a favor to me for coming here, you can at least sit while I eat."

Sighing, she agreed.

"What do you see in these?" He grabbed one showing a guy wearing jeans and chaps and a woman spilling half out of her prairie dress.

She dived for another book. "Adventure, a smidge of history and loads of romance."

Making a face, he noted, "Couldn't you have all of that with a real-live man instead of just reading about it?"

"I don't have time for a real man."

He gave her a dirty look.

"Except, of course, for you."

"That's better."

"Seriously, though…" Her latest pick featured a castle. "Until I have a spare moment for real-life romance, books carry me through. You might give them a try."

"Me?" He laughed. "I could have a date in the next hour."

"True, but with someone you wholly want to be with? A woman who feeds your mind and spirit? Do you plan on spending the rest of your life in pursuit of the eternal party?"

Hell, yes. Since when had fun been declared a bad thing? "What's it matter to you?" he said. "You'll soon be gone. Besides, you don't even know me."

"What little I do know, I discovered on a one-night stand."

"And seems to me you weren't opposed to our night."

"I never said I was." Blushing furiously, she looked away. "All I meant was that sooner or later, that kind of outing will eventually lose its thrill."

He coughed. "Speak for yourself."

Though he'd been teasing, Wren didn't look amused. "You know what I mean."

He did, but since he had no intention of marrying, he failed to see how in his case a lofty ideal such as finding a woman to feed his mind and soul applied.

Clearing his throat, he asked, "We about done here?"

"SURE YOU'RE UP FOR THIS?" Sunday afternoon on their way into Cash's mother's home, he took her hand for a brief squeeze. Though there hadn't been tension between them, there also hadn't been a whole lot of meaningful conversation since their library trek. The hour drive to Tulsa to visit Cash's neighbor, Delores, had been even worse.

"Yeah, I'm good." Forcing a deep breath, Wren tried believing her words. Truth was, her stomach was in knots, her ankles were swollen and more than anything she'd have liked to be lounging by the pool with her latest read. While Doc Haven hadn't placed her on total bed rest, the worse she felt, the more she feared losing her last bit of independence.

"You don't look it."

"Thanks." Just what she needed was Mr. Handsome to confirm her suspicion that she looked like crap. Though she'd been with Cash nearly two weeks, she hadn't encountered his mother again. The thought of the older woman once again urging her to marry, to enter into a lifelong relationship with a man she hardly knew, was too much to comprehend. Wren understood that in sharing a child, she and Cash would be irrevocably linked, but that was vastly different from being legally linked.

"Hey..." He drew her into a hug. "You're beautiful. Really, truly pretty. I just meant that I can tell you're having a rough day."

She tried pushing him away, but he held firm. "You're not going anywhere until you slow down your breathing. Are you really this upset over sharing a meal with my family?"

"Yes—no," she said against his chest. "I don't understand why I'm reacting like this. My heart's beating a mile a minute and..." She held on to him for dear life.

"It's okay. Everything's going to be fine."

"I don't know why, but your mom's opinion means

something to me. It makes no sense. I've never had parents, so why would I care what your mother thinks?"

His fingers gentle beneath her chin, he raised her gaze to meet his. "Mom told me that—"

"You and your mother talked about me?" Horrified didn't begin to cover the emotions surging through her.

"Relax. She understands how important our baby is to you—that you'll finally have a family. Do you think seeing me close to my family has stirred up feelings for you?"

"I don't know... Maybe. I just want to feel normal again, but the more pregnant I get, the more messed up I seem to be."

"You do a good job of hiding it." He kissed her forehead. "Most days you only seem mildly crazy—nowhere near certifiable."

Growling, she tried pushing away again, but he wasn't letting go. And, oddly enough, though she'd never verbally admit it, she didn't want him to.

"So here Cash was," Cash's oldest brother, Dallas, said to their middle brother, Wyatt, "drunk off what had to have been half a keg when he..."

Georgina leaned toward Wren. "How about we leave my boys to their tall tales while we go for a garden stroll?"

"Uh, okay." After enduring a family meal including Dallas's rambunctious five-year-old twin girls and their nanny, the last thing Wren needed was more awkward conversation.

Trailing after the Buckhorn matriarch, Wren focused on slowing her pulse. As long as she held firm to her convictions, nothing Georgina said could hurt her. She was a grown woman with every right to live her life as she wanted.

Exiting the home through French doors transported Wren to a world that felt more like a European wonderland than Oklahoma. Everywhere she looked were roses and ivy-covered trellises and gurgling fountains. The sweet scent of snapdragons mingled with freshly cut grass so lush it could've been living velvet.

"Aside from my kids and grandbabies," Georgina said, "this is my passion. It gets so dry here in the summer that sometimes I water three times a day. Dallas says if there's ever another Oklahoma dust bowl my garden will be to blame."

"It's amazing," Wren said, fighting a childlike urge to kick off her shoes and run barefoot down winding stone paths. "Outside coffee-table books, I've never seen anything like it."

Pausing at a covered seating area featuring wicker rockers with sunny yellow cushions, Georgina gestured for Wren to have a seat.

After a few moments of awkward silence, Georgina said, "Cash informed me I owe you an apology."

"Oh?" Fussing with her fingers, Wren wasn't sure what else to say.

"It seems I overstepped my boundaries when I cornered you about marrying my son. The bribery also wasn't one of my prouder moments." For the longest time she stared off into space. When next she spoke, her voice was raspy, as if she held back tears. "But you have to understand that this baby you're carrying represents a part of my husband. A man I loved to a degree I'd never dreamed possible. The thought of you bringing this precious child into the world, and me never getting to see him or her, well..." Cash's mother no longer bothered trying to hide her pain. "I—I know you and my son hardly know each other, but if you could just find it in your heart to let Cash in, I'm sure..."

Wren stood. "I'm sorry, Mrs. Buckhorn, but I can't do this. Cash and I have already told you we have no intention of marrying, and for you to press the issue is upsetting."

"The idea of you taking off halfway across the country with my grandchild is abhorrent."

"Again, I'm sorry. It's not my intention to keep this baby from you. You're welcome to visit any time you like."

"It's not the same as if you and the baby lived with Cash. If you won't marry, would you consider staying in Weed Gulch?"

Hands over her womb, Wren struggled for words.

How did she begin explaining to her child's grandmother why she needed to keep her distance? Yes, back in Baltimore she had her residency, but technically, she could complete that in almost any large city. As much as she craved family, a part of Wren feared it—not having her own baby, but the notion that if she were to one day marry, her husband's folks might not find her worthy of their son. If that happened, what if he abandoned her just as her parents had? Her heart couldn't bear finally finding people with whom she could find a home, only to lose them. It would be unfathomably cruel. Which was why Wren had long ago decided never to entertain the thought.

Chapter Six

"Daddy says you've got a baby in there."

Wren had made slow progress on the short walk back to Cash's house, only to encounter the look-alike girls she'd first met that afternoon in the Buckhorn dining room.

"I think it's a girl baby." Betsy, the one wearing a purple My Little Pony shirt, performed a pirouette on the driveway.

"It could be a boy baby," Bonnie said. Wren recognized her because of the pink Hello Kitty T-shirt she wore.

"What if it's an alien in there?" Betsy giggled.

The ridiculous question coaxed Wren's smile out of hiding. "I've thought of that," she teased. "If I did have an alien, I'd want it to have polka-dotted skin."

Both girls took a minute to let this sink in.

"Cool!" Betsy said.

"Yeah!" Bonnie skipped in a circle.

"You two always have this much energy?" Wren asked, continuing her journey.

"Uh-huh." In unison, they now skipped and hopped.

Just think, in five short years she'd have one of these little walking atoms of her very own.

"Wait up!"

Wren looked behind her to find Cash jogging up the tree-lined driveway. As usual, he favored his right knee. Out of respect for his privacy, she'd stopped questioning him about it, but still wondered about the full extent of what was wrong. And if that was the reason he hadn't been in a rodeo—or even a sponsored media event— since she'd lived in his home.

"Uncle Cash!" The energy balls ran to meet him.

Bonnie said, "Your girlfriend told us she's gonna have an alien baby with polka dots and green-and-purple blood."

"That so?" Cash scooped up both girls, charging with them squealing all the way to where Wren stood smiling.

"For the record," she noted, giving both girls noogies, "I never said that about the blood."

"With these two—" Cash set them down "—I've gotten used to there being more fiction than fact."

"Give us another ride," Betsy demanded.

"No way. Uncle Cash is broken. Ask your dad to saddle up your ponies."

"Okay!" As suddenly as they'd arrived, the duo was now dashing off for a new adventure.

"Those two are a mess." Cash fell into step with Wren.

"I didn't want to ask at dinner, but where's their mom?"

"Family graveyard. Died in labor."

"Wow." Heat rushed through her. From what she'd read, giving birth was like landing a plane. A delicate process that usually went well, but sometimes horribly wrong. "Wish I hadn't asked."

"Was a freak thing. She started bleeding and didn't stop. Dallas was destroyed. He and Bobbie Jo were together for as long as I can remember. Literally since like the sixth grade."

"I can't imagine surviving such a loss." Which proved Wren's point that giving your heart was more likely to cause harm than good.

"You scared about the baby's grand entry?" On the tail end of his question, Cash caught her gaze.

A part of her wanted to be truthful that, yes, she was terrified of not only the birthing process, but everything that came after. Having had no mother of her own, would she instinctively know how to care for their child? Another part of her thought it best that she follow her long-standing rule of keeping her most private thoughts inside. That way, when she and Cash went their separate ways, he wouldn't keep part of her with him.

"I'm taking your silence as an affirmative." Casually resting his arm across her shoulders, he gave her a squeeze. "Sorry I told you about Bobbie Jo. Should've kept it to myself."

"That's okay. It's not like I haven't learned people die."

"True." When he released her, for a split second she was lonely. Then she regained her senses.

They walked for a few minutes in companionable silence, listening to wind whisper through tall grasses. Oklahoma had a grandeur she hadn't been prepared for. Rolling, cattle-dotted hills that stretched all the way to the horizon. The sun was setting, making the September air nippy while at the same time washing the sky in a hundred shades of orange, lavender and gold.

Had she and Cash been a couple, now would've been the perfect time to snuggle against him, sharing his warmth.

"I'm almost afraid to ask," Cash said once they were almost to the house. "But what did my mother have to say out in her garden? I wanted to warn you that nothing good ever comes from conversations held out there, but Dallas and Wyatt wouldn't let me get a word in edgewise."

"They're a couple of characters."

He chuckled. "That's putting it mildly. But back to Mom…"

"Same CD, different track. If I can't bring myself to marry you, she wants me to at least move to Weed Gulch."

"How are you supposed to finish your residency here?" He mounted the wide slate steps leading to the front door.

"My point exactly. My mentor, Dr. West, has said she'll help me return to the program, but if I'm not in her hospital, I doubt knowing her will pull much weight."

"You'll work it out. I have faith in you."

His words warmed her heart. Wren stood staring at Cash until he held open the door, gesturing for her to enter first.

It felt good to be back. The house had become her haven, with its soaring ceilings and walls of glass. Scents of lemon oil and the lingering fragrance of whatever Mrs. Cahwood had cooked for dinner. The housekeeper was typically in and out before Wren had even showered. Ever since moving in with Cash, her usually frenetic pace had become downright decadent. She now read exclusively for pleasure, snacked and lounged. At first her new routine had felt like a hard-won vacation, but lately she'd grown a little bored and frustrated. She struggled to squelch the constant feeling that she should be doing something more productive than resting.

"It's chilly," Cash said. "Want me to build a fire and you pick a movie?"

"Sounds nice." A wonderful departure from worrying about their baby's delivery or Cash's scowling mother. "I haven't seen a movie in probably a year."

"Really?" At the hearth he meticulously laid a kindling base, setting larger sticks atop that and finally adding a couple of logs. "Dallas's kid duo conned me into a Disney marathon a few weeks back." After striking a match, he eased it under the smallest twigs, soon immersing the room in a dancing glow.

His every movement mesmerized her. He was so capable and sure. Granted, he'd only built a fire, but with all her book smarts, it wasn't something she could do.

Staring into the flames, he said, "Don't tell anyone, but *Pocahontas* and *Beauty and the Beast* were pretty damned good."

Wren laughed. "Afraid you might tarnish your manly-man image?"

"Never." His cocky grin convinced her all was well when it came to his ego. "I just want to ensure those little monsters don't make a habit of crashing at Uncle Cash's. Took me a couple days to fish all the Gummi Bears out of my furniture."

"Betsy and Bonnie are adorable. What're you talking about?"

"Don't let those sweet facades fool you." He

parked himself on the opposite end of the sofa to her. "Well?"

"What?" When he smiled, she lost track of time. The man was so handsome, it hurt.

"I did my part for the evening's entertainment. Where's our movie?"

Yawning, she admitted, "I forgot. You pick."

"Woman…" He rolled his eyes. "I suppose you want me to make that popcorn for you, too?"

Beaming up at him, she said, "Now that you mention it, that would be—oh."

"What's wrong?"

"Nothing." Hands over her belly, she said, "The baby's feeling his oats. I think he just took out one of my ribs."

"Mind if I…" He cautiously approached, holding out his right hand as if he wanted to feel the phenomenon for himself, but was afraid to ask.

Snagging Cash's wrist, Wren drew him close, placing his large hand on her stomach. Within a few seconds their baby kicked again.

"Holy crap…" Eyes wide, he shook his head. "Does that hurt?"

She shook her head. "Usually just feels funny—like an inside tickle."

Sitting on the sofa beside her, he now had both hands over her belly. When the baby kicked again and again, Cash grinned and said, "Screw the movie. Our kid is way more entertaining."

Funny, she was just thinking the same thing about him.

"You're glowing," he said, holding her gaze the way he had in Vegas. With just a look, he stripped her bare.

Made her long for an indefinable something she knew she shouldn't crave. "Crazy beautiful is what you are and I'm going to kiss you."

She should have stopped him, but when he slipped his left hand under her hair with his right still hugging their baby, denial was an impossibility. He kissed her softly and then hard and then every way in between. He stroked her tongue and then lifted her on top of him, urging her legs apart to straddle his waist. With her knees pressing into the soft sofa cushions, an infinitely more sensitive area sat atop throbbing proof of his still-thriving attraction for her.

When she moaned, he eased his hands under her shirt, smoothing her back while bucking in a slow and easy rhythm old as time.

Voice raspy, Cash asked, "What'd the doc say about us makin' whoopee?"

"I—I never thought to ask."

"Yeah, well, you should…." He kissed her a few more times. "But until you find out, you're going to have to excuse me before all the gentleman in me runs out."

"OUCH. LOOKS LIKE YOU got up on the wrong side of the bed."

The next morning, tired and cranky after an exhausting night spent wide awake and lusting, the last person Wren wanted to see was Georgina, but there she stood in all of her towering, Buckhorn glory at the open front door.

"Good thing I brought fiber muffins. They'll perk you right up." Bustling past Wren, the older woman strode to the kitchen, setting a cloth-covered basket on the granite counter. Over her shoulder she'd slung a large bag, the contents of which she'd yet to reveal. "I don't know about you, but every time I got pregnant, my body played a new trick. With Cash, my lower tummy refused to play nice. My mother—bless her soul—made me this recipe and it always did the trick."

"Um, thank you." Was she truly standing in the kitchen talking about an insanely personal issue with a woman she hardly knew?

"My pleasure," Cash's mom said. "Now, let's get you back on the sofa, where I'm going to teach you to needlepoint."

"That's an awfully nice offer," Wren said, already tired from the short walk, "but I'm clueless when it comes to crafts."

"Needlepoint isn't a craft," she said, shooing Wren back to her blanketed sofa nest, "but a womanly art. Next time you're over for dinner, I want you to get a good look at the dining-room chairs. My ancestors stitched every one of the cushions."

"Seriously?" Wren had heard of such things—families holding on to those kind of priceless antiques—but she'd never seen them.

"Of course I'm serious. And trust me, you'd be better off starting on your first project before the baby comes. Once your little bundle of energy arrives, your life will never be the same."

"HAVEN'T SEEN MUCH OF YOU lately." Dallas did a head count of the cattle in the northeast pasture. Usually Wyatt would step in to help their oldest brother, but he'd taken a sick calf into town to the vet.

"Been busy." Cash tipped his hat brim in an attempt to keep cold rain from his eyes. It was a miserable morning to be a working cowboy. Especially after the three long, miserable nights he'd spent horny for the woman sleeping in the room across the hall. Damn, but his baby's mama was a sexy little thing.

Since feeling their baby kick, Cash had made a conscious effort to keep her smiling. They'd made another library run and a trip to the grocery store to stock up on the purple grapes and Doritos she'd been craving. He'd even put wildflowers in a vase on her nightstand. Truth was, the mother of his child was growing on him—figuratively and literally!

From the first time she'd placed his hand on her belly, it was as if he'd been possessed with thoughts of not only her, but their child. Were they having a boy or a girl? Would he or she be healthy? Would Wren's blood pressure remain normal?

As Dallas logged the count with wax pencil on a laminated chart, Cash wondered how he kept his head from exploding with all his efficiency. Their father had never relied on charts or graphs. He'd stored everything upstairs.

Reining his mount toward the northwest pasture, Dallas asked, "What have you been doing? Wyatt says you've been slacking on your rehabilitation. You told us you'd be back on tour in a couple weeks. I realize Wren's been a distraction, but Wyatt figures you've missed at least three stops and enough sponsor events to get yourself fired."

"Wyatt needs to mind his own business."

"Sorry to break it to you, but you are our business.

Mom's pushing me over the edge with nagging." He snorted. "Not only is she worried about your knee, but she thinks I can shame you into giving Wren and your baby your name."

"Stop. When you called at an ungodly hour asking for help today, I didn't think your ulterior motive was to ambush me."

"More like talk sense into you. The clock's ticking and before you know it, this baby will be here and gone. That what you really want?"

Approaching a steep slope, forcing his attention to directing his horse, Cash wasn't sure what he wanted other than for Dallas to shut his piehole. "Look, Wren's my business. As is *my* kid."

"That's where you're wrong. This child is a Buckhorn, and don't you forget it." Dallas's horse turned skittish at his harsh tone. "First and foremost, you are to remember your family name. When Dad died, he left me in charge, and I refuse to allow you to bring scandal upon his legacy."

"For God's sake," Cash shouted back at his big brother, "would you please step out of the Old West and into the new millennium? Obviously I have no business being a husband or father. Yes, I'll be sad when Wren takes the baby with her, but what if I'm also relieved? Did you ever think of that?"

"If I weren't mounted, I'd slug you right in the jaw." As the rain fell harder, Dallas worked his fists. "Can you even imagine what my girls have been through not having their mother? All the time, they're asking me girl stuff for which I don't have answers. What is your son or daughter going to do when they have questions?

What's the reason Wren's going to give them for why their daddy stays away? No, he's not in heaven, just too caught up in his own good time to give a damn about his offspring."

"THIS IS DELICIOUS, Mrs. Cahwood. Thank you." While the housekeeper hovered, Wren pressed a napkin to her lips. Back in Baltimore, breakfast consisted of an energy bar. If she were really lucky, she might also have time for yogurt or a banana. "You're spoiling me."

The perpetually cheerful older woman shrugged. With her hair in a messy French twist and usual white blouse always paired with pearls, she'd have been a dead ringer for June Cleaver if she hadn't also habitually worn blue jeans. "I like spoiling you. Plus, it'll be nice having a little one around the house."

Wren's stomach sank. Was it a middle-America thing that had everyone in her current circle assuming that just because she carried Cash's baby they'd be together forever?

She finished her latest strip of turkey bacon. "I guess Cash hasn't told you, but after I have the baby, I'll be moving back to Baltimore. I need to finish my residency."

"But isn't that very time-consuming?" The woman quickened her pace on wiping the counters. "Who will watch your child? I have four, and trust me, that first one sucks the life right out of you."

"The hospital where I'll be working has an excellent day care. Plus, my mentor, Dr. West, has more contacts than anyone I've ever known. She's already offered to help."

"I understand that sort of thing if you have no other

option, but when you have a built-in support system right here in Weed Gulch, why would you want to leave?"

She made it sound so simple. As if giving up on a goal she'd worked her entire life to achieve was no big deal. "Please don't take this the wrong way, but did you ever want more from life? Something other than caring for your own or someone else's home?"

"Sure. Believe it or not," she said with a pat to her ample behind, "I dreamed of becoming a Rockette. I did it, too."

"Really?" Wren was so surprised she dropped her toast.

"You don't have to look so shocked."

"Sorry. I just never would've suspected it."

Brandishing still long and lean legs, Mrs. Cahwood said, "I danced in a reunion show just last year. A lot of my old friends got caught up in reminiscing, wishing they could be back in the limelight. But you know what I remember most about that time?"

Leaning forward, Wren asked, "Adoring fans? Gorgeous costumes?"

"Nope. I could never stop thinking about home. How much I missed my mom and dad and kid sister. I'd obtained something I'd worked for since my first dance class when I was only three years old, but without anyone there to share it with me, my victory felt hollow. Once my contract was up, I got a bank loan and set up my own little dance studio here in Weed Gulch. Turns out I loved teaching dance just as much as performing. Sure, it wasn't anywhere near as flashy, but as I got older, my values changed. I discovered true happiness wasn't in achieving an end goal, but in the journey."

Slipping the bacon pan into the sink, she added, "You might think about that next time you're daydreaming about returning to the big city."

Chapter Seven

Thursday afternoon Cash had finished his chores and found Wren reading by the pool. It was a gorgeous afternoon. Bright and sunny with temperatures in the mid-eighties. Perfect for drowning out Dallas's condemning speech with fun. "Wanna join me for a swim?"

"Love to," she said, "but I don't have a maternity suit."

"How's that a problem?" He grinned. "Especially when God made you a perfectly fine birthday suit."

She rolled her eyes. "I thought until the doctor clears me for, um, *action*, we weren't going to do any more of that kind of activity?"

"Lord, woman, I didn't say I was makin' love to you in the pool. I'd just be getting an eyeful. Hell, if you want, I'll let you look at me right now." And to prove it, he unbuttoned his trunks.

"Stop!" she screeched with her book over her eyes.

"Okay, but if you ever want a peek, all you have to do is ask." When he winked, her face turned red as a beet. "Until then, come on, let's get you something pretty. There's a specialty shop over in Fouke. I'll bet they have something big enough to fit."

"Beast!" She threw her book at him. "First you want to see me naked, now you're calling me fat?"

"Never." Leaning low to kiss her, he said, "Sorry if it came out wrong. I realize my big baby boy is making your stomach huge."

"Like that sounds any better?"

"Whatever. I'm sorry if I offended you. Bottom line, it's a freakishly gorgeous day and I don't want to swim alone. Now, will you go shopping with me? Or is your refusal a subtle way of telling me you'd rather skinny-dip?"

IMPOSSIBLE DIDN'T BEGIN to describe Cash.

An hour had passed since his raunchy suggestion and Wren now stood in the dressing room of Fouke's Baby Barn. Surveying her image in the mirror, she wasn't sure if the pink floral suit made her look more like a cartoon hippo or a funky lounge chair. Either way, she wasn't wearing the getup in public any time soon.

"Does it fit?" Cash asked. He'd insisted on occupying the chair right outside her room.

"Technically, yes. But that—"

The dressing-room door creaked open. "Damn, woman…" Cash's smiling image appeared in the mirror alongside hers. "You look hot."

"Get out!" she snapped, grabbing for the white T-shirt she'd worn to at least partially cover herself.

"Have you seen the size of your—" At least having the decency to redden, he cleared his throat. "Suffice to say, our baby will be well fed."

To heck with modesty. She straightened her shoulders, giving him a real eyeful of her newly enlarged *assets*. "It's a shame you'll miss the party."

"Woman," he said with a growl, "I *am* the party." His agility meant he'd easily drawn her in for another kiss. "Shoot, if you weren't already having my baby, I might hire you for the job."

"Stop!" she begged in a stage whisper. "You're making a scene."

"So are you with your baby-enhanced boobs." After a quick check over his shoulder to make sure no one was looking, he ducked into the already cramped room.

"What are you doing?"

Easing his hands around her, smoothing them in a lazy up-and-down motion that did wild things to her pulse, he said, "What's it feel like I'm doing?"

"Wreaking havoc?"

"I should hope so." He focused on her neck, nuzzling and kissing and flooding Wren's body with aching, forbidden want.

"Really," she said, pushing him back the whole four inches the space allowed, "you have to stop."

"Why? It's not like we haven't already done all of this and more."

"I know, but…" It felt so good being back in his arms. Oddly right. What would it hurt indulging in this little bit of pleasure?

What would it hurt?

Try everything!

Not only didn't they have Doc Haven's safety clearance, but she had way too much at stake to risk losing it all on a casual affair. Getting pregnant had been bad enough. As much as she now wanted her baby, she was that much afraid of how she'd manage being a good mother and a doctor. No way could she toss being a good *girlfriend* for Cash into the mix.

Cash sidled right back beside her. "Just one kiss," he whispered, his breath warm and moist in her ear.

A knock sounded on the dressing-room door. "Is anyone in here?"

Heart pounding, Wren answered, "Um, yes! A-almost done."

"Just one," he urged, lips hot against the base of her throat. "Promise, if it's that awful, you can pretend you've never met me."

"Need any other sizes?" the sales clerk persisted.

"N-no, thank you."

"You know you want me." His raspy whisper caused hot and cold shivers. Of course she wanted him. *Want* wasn't the point. Sanity dictated she keep her distance. A repeat of their Vegas adventure would only make it tougher for her to eventually say goodbye. "C'mon…"

Glancing into his green eyes was her undoing. Everything about him invited her in. He represented the world of forbidden pleasure she'd spent her lifetime working to resist. Chocolate and staying up too late and dating rather than becoming one with her anatomy tomes.

"I—I want to," she said, licking her lips, "but…"

Kisses on her forehead, her cheek, the palm of her hand gave her only a sampling of what he ultimately offered.

"Ma'am?" The sales clerk rapped again. "If you're finished, we have a line waiting for the room."

"All right," Wren answered.

Cash made a face toward the door.

Abandoning her logical side, Wren slipped her hands behind Cash's head and pressed her lips to his. It took everything in her not to groan, and when he eased his hands under the top of her tankini-style suit, skimming them along her sides, teasing the sensitive skin near her breasts, she feared her legs would crumple from pleasure.

"Need help getting out of that sexy thing?" Cash teased.

Thank heavens they were in a public setting or she might've taken him up on his latest offer.

"Ma'am?" The clerk's tone had turned sharp. "Is someone in there with you?"

When Cash launched into a fresh set of mocking faces, Wren couldn't hold back a giggle, which quickly turned into a laugh.

Snatching the tag from her suit, Cash opened the door. "We'll take it," he said, handing the clerk what she'd need to ring up Wren's purchase.

Wren cringed in horror, tugging the door closed before dragging her shirt and maternity jeans on over the ugly suit.

Leaving the room with her bra shoved into her purse, Wren strove for a devil-may-care attitude on her walk of shame past the gaping crowd of moms and grandmothers. A scowling grandfatherly type clamped his hands over a squirming toddler's eyes. Wren opted for the long route to the front of the store, zigzagging through clothing racks and a towering infant car seat display to eventually stand alongside Cash.

"Will the swimwear be all?" The clerk glared at them over the top of her reading glasses.

"Sweetheart," Cash said to Wren, kissing the crown of her head, "need anything else? Thongs? Bras? Guess there's no need for condoms."

"Sir," the clerk admonished, handing Cash his change, "this is a family establishment."

"And clearly," Cash said with a pat to Wren's tummy along with his trademark grin, "we're in a family way."

"YOU'RE AWFUL," WREN noted an hour later while lounging on a hot-pink air mattress in the center of the pool.

"I'm also the one who made your current comfort level possible."

"That may well be, but as long as I live, I'll never get that clerk's horrified features from my mind."

He dived under the heated water, popping up alongside her. "Admit it, that was the most fun you've had in a while, if not ever."

In the glare, all she could focus on was the white of his smile and water beads gathering on his muscular, sun-kissed skin. Mouth dry, she managed, "I will admit nothing."

"Because you're ashamed of craving more of the same?" He formed a cup with his hands, scooping water into them and trailing it over her overheated chest. "It's okay to admit. Promise, I won't turn you down."

Lips pursed, she sighed. "What's wrong with you? In a single day you've transformed from all-around good guy to raving horndog."

"It's your fault," he complained, "parading around with your *goodies* on display."

"My *goodies* were safely tucked away in a dressing room!" Rolling off her pool toy with as much grace as she could muster considering she carried her own built-in floatie, Wren sloshed toward the shallow-end stairs.

Unfortunately, Cash followed. "I'm sorry, okay?"

Out of the pool, she took her towel from a lounger, wrapping it sarong-style—only, it didn't cover her bulging belly. Great.

Hands over her shoulders, causing unwitting havoc with the simplest of touches, he said, "Guess I've gotten used to having you around. I don't know if it's the unseasonably warm weather or what, but it felt good not worrying about anything and just having fun. I should be working my knee. I need to make amends with my mom, and now Dallas."

"What's wrong with him?"

Cash released her, slicking the water from his hair. "What's that expression you used? Same CD, different track?"

"That's the one." Taking another towel from the pile Mrs. Cahwood had thoughtfully set outside, Wren put it around her still-tingling shoulders.

Perching on a low rock wall, he said, "I get where they're coming from—the whole give-our-baby-the-Buckhorn-name thing. But it's not like you don't see Hollywood types not marrying."

"Considering where you live and your family's standing within the community, I wouldn't expect that argument to hold water."

"That's such B.S." Now pacing, he said, "My big brother is well on his way to following in our dad's footsteps, as is Wyatt, but I've always been a disappointment."

"I don't believe that for a second." Wren's heart went out to him. All her life she'd wished for a family, but never once had she considered the pressure of living up to their expectations. "You're a rodeo star. Every ranch needs one of those."

"Mom and Dad dreamed of me becoming a veterinarian. What I do is a far cry from that."

Not thinking, just following her gut feelings, Wren went to him, wrapping her arms around him for a hug. "What you do is entertain everyone who sees you. You give them an escape from their everyday drudgery. If your mom and brothers don't see the importance in making people smile, then that's their problem."

"Who knew I had a little scrapper living with me?" He kissed the tip of her nose.

"First off, there's nothing *little* about me. Second, I'm not sure what I expected to find just dropping in on you like I did, but in light of the circumstances, you've been as welcoming as anyone could be."

"Thanks. Coming from you, that means a lot."

"Why from me?"

Releasing her to pace again, he said, "You're a family virgin."

"A what?"

"You know, since you haven't had a real, blood-related family, you don't know what a pain in the ass they can be. Which is one more reason why for us, marrying would be stupid."

But we're not blood related. The only thing linking them was smoking-hot chemistry.

A fact she'd be better off forgetting.

Chapter Eight

"Am I cleared?" Cash winced while hopping off the exam table in the National Bull Riding Team's Dallas facility.

His longtime friend and team doctor, Mack Duggan, consulted MRI images on a computer screen. "'Fraid not."

"Why? I've rested for six weeks."

"Right, and I told you after that time we'd take another MRI and reassess. Bottom line, just as I'd suspected, you have a nasty anterior cruciate ligament tear and I'm not clearing you to rejoin the tour until you've had corrective surgery. Even then—" he patted Cash's back "—there are no guarantees."

Though in his heart Cash had feared the news had been coming, that didn't make it easier to stomach. Slamming the nearest wall with the heel of his right hand, he said, "Dammit, I don't need this right now. Can't I just man up and deal with the pain?"

Making notes on Cash's chart, Mack said, "If you want me to lose my job. C'mon, work with me. Have the surgery. We're talking six months recovery max, and then we'll reassess."

With a sarcastic snort, Cash added, "Yeah, with pissed-off sponsors and no income."

"Look," his friend said, "you've already earned more at rodeo than a lot of people do in a lifetime. You're a young man. This isn't a death sentence. Worst case scenario, a possible change in your life's course."

Cash's drive home was long.

He was used to a lot of time on the road. What he wasn't accustomed to was having his mind run faster than his truck's engine.

News that he'd have to go under the knife wasn't what most bothered him. It was the fact that on the off chance the surgery didn't go well, he might never ride again, at least not at a professional level. Screw the money—time on the road was his lifeblood. It was the only place he got validation that he was okay. He sure as hell didn't hear that news from Dallas or his mother. Yes, he was a screwup with women, but he'd always been a phenomenal bull rider. No matter what, he'd always had that to fall back on for all of his financial and emotional needs.

Without it, where did that leave him?

Worse yet, he had the added worry of sweet, funny, very pregnant Wren. Was she faring all right on her own? If he went under the knife ASAP, who would care for her then?

True, Mrs. Cahwood handled the household feeding and cleaning, but Wren needed rides to the library and plenty of chocolate-dipped cones at Queenie's. Who would make sure Wren didn't capsize in the pool or always had fresh wildflowers on her nightstand?

By the time he'd turned onto the road leading to his home, it was well past midnight. He'd expected the house to be dark, but lamplight shone through the windows, and on the couch he saw Wren curled up with one of her books. The sight of her warmed him. Made him feel oddly whole. As if even though his professional life was quite possibly shot to hell, everything would turn out all right.

Out of the truck, knee throbbing, Cash tried shaking out the stiffness. As usual, it didn't work. But for once, mounting the porch steps, the pain was okay. For better or worse, it was part of him. Just like the woman waiting up for him inside.

"Did you win?" Wren asked, sleepy eyed and hair tousled. She rested her book atop her baby bulge.

"Nah." He'd told her he'd spent the day competing. He hadn't needed her questions or pity. Now he almost wished he'd taken her with him. She'd have been able to not only explain the medical implications of surgery, but alleviate his no doubt irrational fears of possibly never riding bulls again. "Didn't even place."

"I'm sorry." Rising, she slipped her arms around him for a hug. "Mrs. Cahwood made blackberry cobbler. Want me to warm you a piece?"

"Sounds delicious," he said, nuzzling her sweet-smelling dark waves. "Do we have ice cream?"

She laughed. "That's like asking if I'm ever up all night, peeing."

Trailing her into the kitchen, he settled in at the table, appreciating her curves while she bustled to prepare his snack. "I should be waiting on you."

"Give me a break," she said with a pretty grin in his direction. "I've been sitting all day. It feels good to be productive."

While the cobbler was being nuked, she smoothed

the hair back from his forehead, rubbing his temples and then aching shoulders. "You're one big knot."

"Tell me about it."

Still kneading, she asked, "What can I get you to drink?"

"Shot of Jim Beam."

She leaned over to view his expression. "Seriously?"

"Better make it two."

"All right…" Ignoring the beeping microwave, Wren pulled out a chair and tried straddling it, but her belly got in the way. "Rats." Once she turned the seat back around and plopped down in the usual way, she said, "Pardon that brief interruption. Now, what happened that's got you turning to drink? Did you get hurt physically, or is this an ego thing?"

Should he tell her the truth?

"Cash?" Her eyes begged him to let her in, but was he strong enough? If she knew all of his secrets and fears, what else stood between them to keep their attraction at bay?

Leaning into her, he rested his head atop their baby. "I'm sorry. I lied about where I've been."

The color drained from her face. "Were you with another woman?"

"What?" Raising his head, he took her hands. "Trust me, it's nothing like that. Why would that even cross your mind?"

"I don't know." She lowered her gaze. "It's stupid— and none of my business. If you want to be with somebody, then…"

He kissed her. Nothing fancy or calculated to make

her want more, but brimming with emotion straight from his heart. "You've been on my mind all day."

Hands to her lips, she said, "You shouldn't have done that."

"I know. But how else could I get my point across that there's no other woman?"

"That's *my* point." Taking his cobbler from the microwave, she said, "We don't have that kind of relationship. Because of the baby, we'll always share that connection, but nothing more."

"Why do I get the feeling you're working overtime to convince yourself that's what you want?"

Ice cream in hand, she slammed the freezer door. "I don't know what you're talking about."

"Can we call a truce?" Standing behind her, he pinned her at the counter, fighting his every instinct to nuzzle her neck.

"Fine." After topping his dessert, she pushed him aside to return the frozen treat to the freezer.

"Does that mean you'll share this with me?" Knowing full well she'd never met a sweet she didn't like, he wagged the bowl.

"Thanks, but I'm ready for bed."

So much for telling her why he'd lied. She hadn't even cared. Chalk this up as just one more reason why Cash didn't need a woman in his life.

WREN CLOSED HER BEDROOM door and leaned against it.

"Baby," she whispered, feeling like a fool for talking to her belly, "your father is infuriating. Worse yet, his kisses are dreamier than lemon meringue pie. I've got our whole lives carefully mapped out for us, and nowhere on that map is a sign leading us straight into the arms of a too-handsome-for-his-own-good cowboy."

Her baby kicked.

"Thank you for agreeing."

As Wren readied for bed, the trained doctor in her knew late-night indigestion was what had her baby more active than usual. But she ignored that reasoning in favor of the idea that she and the baby were already emotionally connected.

Worse yet, Cash had admitted to lying about where he'd spent his day, but she'd been so wrapped up in the thought of him being with another woman that she hadn't even asked where he'd been. Not a good thing, considering the multitude of places a man like Cash could find trouble.

"YOU EVER TALKING TO ME again?" In Doc Haven's waiting room Monday morning, Cash slapped down a copy of *People* magazine and glared at Wren.

"Maybe." She didn't bother looking up from her *US Weekly*.

"Let me get this straight," he said in a hushed tone. "You're miffed because I kissed you and you liked it."

"Did not." She tried acting offended, but the underlying flush to her complexion told him he'd pushed the right button.

Doc Haven's nurse opened the exam area's door. "Wren Barnes."

Cash stood along with the mother of his child.

"Oh, no," she whispered. "Don't think for a second you're going back there with me."

"It's my baby and I have every right to hear how *he's* coming along."

"*She's* doing great." The strap to her purse got hung around the chair arm. Cash cheerfully unhooked it for her.

Instead of thanking him, Wren glared harder.

"Good morning," the nurse chirped when they approached. "How's the momma today?"

"Miserable," Wren said with a pained look in Cash's direction.

"Isn't she cute?" Once they'd passed through the door, Cash put his arm around her.

In the exam room, when Cash tried helping Wren onto the bench table, she snapped, "I can do it myself."

"Go for it." He released her, only to quickly see she hadn't a prayer of safely making it without major assistance.

Though she didn't look happy about it, Wren grabbed hold of him, clutching him for support. "Thank you."

"Any time."

The nurse made a note on her chart.

"Miss Barnes, if you'll lend me your arm, I'll go ahead and take your blood pressure."

Wren removed the sweater she'd squeezed into to counteract the October chill. Indian summer was gone, replaced by blustery wind and a cold drizzle. Thrusting out her arm, Wren said, "Do your worst."

"I'll try to be gentle." A few minutes later the woman removed her stethoscope's earpieces and frowned. "One fifty-six over ninety-four."

"That good?" Cash asked.

"No." Wren put her hands to her forehead.

"Is she okay? Do we need to run her to a Tulsa hospital?"

"Not just yet," the nurse assured him. "Let Doc Haven take a look, and I'm sure Mommy and baby will be fine."

After another reassuring smile, the smiley blonde left them on their own.

"Tell it to me straight," Cash said to Wren. "How serious is this?"

She shook her head. "It's probably nothing. Stress related."

"What are you stressed about?"

She crossed her arms, and her scowl hit him like a well-aimed slug.

"Do you even have to ask?"

"Me? You're upset over me?" He laughed. "That's the stupidest thing I've ever heard."

"Maybe to you, but obviously my blood pressure doesn't lie."

Doc Haven bustled into the room. "Sally tells me my favorite patient's vitals aren't ideal?"

"True," Wren said.

"You've been taking it easy? Eating right?"

"Yes and yes," Cash answered.

Extending his hand for Cash to shake, the doctor said, "Nice to see you taking an interest in your future child's health."

What was he supposed to say? *Sure, Doc. Up until now I just didn't give a damn?* Cash had always cared— he just hadn't realized how much.

"Wren, before we snoop on your little guy or gal's heart rate, in general, how have you been feeling? Swelling in your extremities?"

"No." Easing her back on the exam table, the doctor extended it to make room for her dangling feet, and then raised her shirt, exposing Wren's belly. "Nothing out of the ordinary."

She sucked in her breath when he squeezed clear gel from a bottle.

"Cold?"

She nodded.

"Sorry. They make gizmos to heat this gunk, but I haven't gotten around to ordering one." He waved a wand over Wren's belly until all of a sudden a rapid-fire thumping sounded from what looked to Cash like one of the twins' old baby monitors. "Whoa. Sounds like you have a track star growing in there. Nice and strong."

Wren released the breath she'd been holding.

"The next few days," the doctor said, wiping her stomach and then tugging down her shirt, "I'd like you to do better at keeping off your feet as much as possible. Cash, that means whatever this little gal needs, you're to deliver. Ice cream, pickles, late-night fried chicken—within reason, whatever she wants."

"Yessir."

"Also—" the doctor took a tissue from a box on the counter, using it to clean his glasses "—I want you back here Friday. If we don't see an improvement, I'm checking you in to Saint Francis in Tulsa for observation."

Chapter Nine

"Now you simply have to marry her." In the kitchen with her son, Georgina Buckhorn spoke as if Wren wasn't even in the house.

Wren had set up camp on the living-room sofa.

Outside, cold rain had set in and the wind howled, making Wren grateful for the crackling fire Cash had made.

Snuggling deeper into the fuzzy pink blanket he'd brought her, she closed her eyes, inhaling deeply through her nose and exhaling through her mouth.

"God forbid, what if something happens? What if that poor little baby is stillborn without ever having had a proper name?"

"Mom," Cash said, clanking around in the kitchen, "Wren isn't supposed to be upset. If you won't let this go, you'll have to leave."

Georgina lowered her voice to the point Wren could no longer hear.

Eyes wide open, she fought to achieve the comfort level she'd found before Cash's mother had stopped by for a supposedly friendly chat.

Cash appeared, carrying a plateful of the turkey-and-

Swiss sandwiches Mrs. Cahwood had left for lunch. His smile was forced.

His mother marched behind him with sliced apples and bananas as if Wren were a toddler incapable of chewing whole food. "Here you go," she said, setting her load on the coffee table. "All nice and healthy for you. Lots of fiber, too." She winked.

"Thanks."

The older woman had brought an extra plate and now assembled snack-sized portions she handed to Wren. "When I carried Wyatt, I was perpetually hungry. His sister, not so much." Fleetingly enough as to make Wren wonder if she might've imagined it, a wistful look saddened Mrs. Buckhorn's features. "First losing your father, then Daisy... When you get to be my age, multiple losses seem to exponentially increase heartache."

"You talk as if she's dead, Mom." Cash grabbed a sandwich. "My gut tells me Daisy's great—just for her own reasons choosing to live on her own."

Hands to her temples, Wren said, "If you all don't mind, I think I'll go to my room and have a nap."

"I've upset you, haven't I?" Fussing with Wren's still-full plate, Cash's mother dabbed her napkin at a few crumbs on the table. "It's just that with my daughter Lord-only-knows where, and now my future grandchild about to meet the same fate..." Hand to her chest, she dragged in a breath and shuddered. "It's oftentimes more than I can bear."

"Quit being melodramatic." Cash slammed his plate on the table and was on his feet, pacing before the windows. "You hate losing control."

"I didn't raise you to be cruel."

Turning to her, he asked, "What did you raise me for?"

Wren cleared her throat. "I—I'm going to give you two some privacy."

"No." When she rose, Cash urged her back down. "Whether we're legally wed or not, you're carrying my child. That makes you family." To his mother, he said, "All my life you and Dad told me what to do. Quit riding bulls. You'll only get hurt. Go to college. Do something valuable with your life. Marry a nice girl. Settle down. Never once in all of those demands did either of you just wish me happiness. Why is that, Mom?"

"What's wrong with you?" With her napkin, Georgina blotted tears from her eyes. "Why are you acting this way?"

Wren resisted the urge to pull the blanket over her head and hide. How long had she dreamed of belonging to a real family? If this was what it was like, then she truly was better off on her own.

"I'm hurt, okay? My riding career might be done. That make you happy? Finally hearing me admit you and Dad were right?"

"Of course not. Your father may have wished you'd chosen a more academic path for your life, but that doesn't mean he wasn't proud of you." His mother tried embracing him, but he nudged her away.

"The team doctor says I have to have surgery. Even then, I might not be cleared to ever rejoin the tour."

"Oh, honey..." She again reached out to hug him, only this time he fell into her arms.

Wren remained frozen on the couch.

Why hadn't Cash shared this with her? Lack of trust? But then, why should he trust her? Aside from sharing great sex, they were practically strangers. Was seeing a specialist what he'd gone to Dallas for?

"If I can't ride again," he asked, "what am I going to do?"

Stepping back, Georgina braced her son's shoulders. "You're going to be the man your father knew you to be. First we'll get you a second—even third—opinion. If all of those doctors are in agreement, you'll face that reality when and if it comes. Until then—" she turned to Wren "—we have much to be thankful for. Together we'll ride out any storm."

"YOU'RE QUIET," CASH said to Wren an hour after his mom had left. Rain still fell, and the KOTV weatherman said by night it could change over to an early snow.

"I'm reading." She didn't look up from her book.

"Must be a good page, seeing how you haven't turned it the whole time I've been sitting here."

Resting the book on the sofa back, she said, "Truthfully, though I understand why you wouldn't confide in me about your knee, I'm hurt. I wouldn't have expected details, but why couldn't you have at least told the truth about your Dallas trip?"

Fear? Embarrassment? Hell if he knew.

"I thought we'd grown close. At least become friends. Now..." She smoothed her hands over their baby. "I have to wonder if I mean anything to you at all. And that seriously messes with my head, considering I've been adamant against us sharing anything beyond the most basic of platonic relationships once our child is born."

Cash added a log to the fire. "Of course we're close. I tried telling you about my Dallas trip, but then we kissed and everything got messed up in my mind. I had this image of me being the perfect guy for you. Making boatloads of money and buying you and our child everything you'd ever need. But if I'm off the tour, all that changes. I'm back to earning a living the old-fashioned way, which is something I've never done."

"Please face me." When he did, she said, "Beyond helping people, a large part of why I wanted to become a doctor was to be self-sufficient. No matter what, as a healer, my services will always be in demand. So as far as money goes, I couldn't care less what you earn or if I ever see a dime of child support. In the short term, I'm dead broke. And because I've been blessed enough to have scholarships that negated the need for student loans, once my residency's over I'll make more than enough to support myself and our baby. The last thing you should worry about is taking care of me."

What if I find myself in the unexpected position of wanting to care for you and our kiddo? Cash wasn't sure how, but Wren had become a lifeline. She was the only thing keeping him sane in his otherwise upside-down world.

"Cash?"

He looked up.

"Talk to me. What's going through that handsome head of yours?"

"Finally admitting it, huh?" With a pinched smile nowhere near as potent as usual, he took one of the sandwiches left to wilt on the coffee table. "I'm the best-looking man you've ever seen?"

"That's a given. What I need you to be is the most communicative."

"GIRL," DELORES HAWKE SAID Friday afternoon at her home's front door, "you've grown big as a house. Get in here before we both catch our death of cold."

Passing Cash's elderly neighbor, Wren barely got around her new aluminum walker. The woman's hip surgery had been a success and after weeks in a convalescent home, she'd been released to care for herself. Cash had taken Wren to visit several times and they'd become fast friends.

At her doctor's appointment that morning, Wren's blood pressure had been back to normal, meaning when she'd heard from Doc Haven that Delores had been sprung, it was the perfect way to celebrate Wren's own good health.

Collapsing onto her new power chair, Delores said, "Be a dear and fetch us some cookies before we settle in for a nice visit. All I have are store bought until I'm back to one hundred percent."

Laughing all the way to the kitchen, Wren hoped she had as much spunk when she was eighty.

Armed with two tumblers filled with milk and two saucers of coconut macaroons, Wren returned to the living room and sat on a loud floral sofa featuring crocheted doilies on the arms and across the back. Cool weather had helped considerably to tame the scent of mothballs and Bengay.

"Where's that man of yours?" Delores asked after downing two cookies and half her milk.

"First, Cash is hardly mine, and second, Dallas sent him to the feed store with a long list. He's picking me up on his way home."

"No wedding bells, then?"

"Not you, too," Wren said with a sigh. "What is it with this town? Everyone's obsessed with marriage."

"Oh, don't go getting your panties twisted." She popped another cookie into her mouth and chewed. "Isolated as we are, Weed Gulch has old-fashioned values. Back when I was your age, an unwed mother would make front-page news. I know, to your generation it sounds crazy, but that's how it was. We had no such thing as divorce statistics, because folks didn't get divorced. More often than not, you grew to love each other. Good or bad, you stayed together until death do you part."

Grinning, Wren had to ask, "So then everyone understood if you ended up killing each other?"

"HAVE A NICE VISIT?" Cash had gone inside to chat with Delores for a short while, but once he'd got wind that the topic centered on marriage, he'd ushered Wren to the door.

"Fine," she said, accepting his help climbing into the truck.

With her safely buckled in, he got behind the wheel, starting the engine for the short ride home.

"How was the feed store?"

"Good. I bought you a present."

"More popcorn?" Since her first batch, she'd taken to having some every afternoon, munching while reading. She usually dropped a bunch, making a hellacious mess wherever she'd happened to park herself.

"Since that's a given—it doesn't count. Guess again."

"I don't know, it's the feed store. A new hoe or rake?"

"Hmm... No and no." He couldn't ever remember being so excited to give someone a gift—not even when he'd made his mother a Popsicle-stick log cabin in 4-H.

"You do know it's not nice to tease pregnant people? We're prone to snap."

He flashed a smile. "I'll take my chances."

The drive time couldn't have been over fifteen minutes, but it felt like an eternity. What would she think? Was his gift too personal? Would she even like it? How could she not? He probably shouldn't have left it in the truck bed, but the woman who'd sold it to him said it would be all right for the short trip.

He stopped in front of the house. "You stay put. And close your eyes. I don't want any peeking."

"Yes, sir," she said with a saucy salute.

"You all right?" Cash asked, scooping the cutie out of her blanket-filled box. The hamster-sized puppy—supposedly a Yorkie-Chihuahua mix—licked his nose.

"Hurry!" Wren shouted. "I have to pee!"

"Your mother's very demanding," Cash whispered, cradling the furball to his chest.

"*Really* bad!"

"How about holding it long enough to meet the newest member of our household." Cupping the puppy in his palms, he presented it to Wren. "Okay, open your eyes."

She did, only her reaction wasn't quite what he'd intended. Instantly tearing, she looked at the puppy for the longest time, then cried, "Cash, how c-could you?"

Now in full-blown sobs, Wren gave the trembling pup one last look before running into the house, slamming the door behind her.

Chapter Ten

Having locked herself in the bathroom for at least twenty minutes, Wren wasn't surprised when Cash pounded on the door.

"Come on, she's just a puppy. How scary can she be?"

"I—I'm not scared," Wren wailed, "but sad."

He persisted. "Same question, different word. She's adorable, not sad."

Wren cried harder.

"Hope you're decent," Cash called, "because like it or not, I'm coming in." The doorknob jiggled and true to his word—albeit with his eyes closed—he barged in. He'd brought the puppy with him, a fact that did little to help Wren's emotional train wreck.

Seated on the tile tub surround, she covered her face with her hands.

Cash knelt in front of her. "Honey, what's wrong?"

"Nothing!" she wailed. *"Everything!"*

"Okay, breathe…" He set the puppy on Wren's baby belly. Lowering her hands, she looked down at the squirming, shivering mess of a tiny dog. It whimpered and looked up at her, melting her into hundreds of shattering pieces. Scooping it up, she cradled it between her breasts, nuzzling the puffy fur between the dog's ears. "Better?"

She nodded. "Sorry. This baby has my emotions all over the map. You couldn't have known."

"That I'm living with a psycho?" He laughed.

Wren didn't.

With Cash stroking her hair and the dog licking her nose with the sweetest puppy breath, had Wren been a cat, she'd have purred.

"I'm kidding," he said, "but when you get a second, I'd love you to let me in on what it was about this goofy-looking dog that sent you over the edge."

"It's stupid. *I'm* stupid for letting something that happened a hundred years ago affect me today."

"You don't look that old." He tugged a lock of her hair.

"I feel it." Yawning, the hamster-sized dog still held close, she asked, "Wanna take this conversation to my bed?"

"Thought you'd never ask."

CASH HAD NEVER SEEN A prettier sight than Wren sleeping with his gift snuggled into the crook of her neck. She'd broken his heart with the story of how she'd found a puppy hiding in the bushes at her orphanage. For weeks she'd secretly fed it and cared for it, visiting every chance she'd gotten. Then she'd been caught sneaking it lunch scraps. By that afternoon, the pound had loaded it into the back of a truck and she'd never seen it again.

Since then, she'd avoided anything with fur like the plague. Fur equaled pain. Though she hadn't said it, he assumed she felt the same way about forging emotional connections.

So that was her reasoning. What was his excuse?

Wren was a great woman. Any man would be thrilled she was having his baby. Any other man would have also long since proposed, but not Cash. No matter how perfect Wren might be, he wasn't the marrying kind.

Didn't have it in him.

"What are you doing?" Wren asked, catching him standing over her.

"Thinking."

"About what?" She yawned, in the process waking the fur ball—who also yawned.

"You two look alike." Both of his girls had crazy bed hair and sleepy eyes.

"I'll take that as a compliment." She gave the dog a rub.

"Got a name for her?"

She took a minute to answer. "I named my first dog Waldo, after the books. I loved them."

"Waldo?" Cash made a face. "Not a very pretty name for such a gorgeous little girl." Snatching the dog for himself, he held her out in front of him, surveying her mutton-chop sideburns.

"How about Wenda?" Wren suggested. "That's his girlfriend's name."

"I thought his girlfriend was Wanda?"

Laughing, she asked, "Got your iPhone? Let's look it up." Ten minutes later they'd discovered Wenda and Wanda were twins. Waldo had officially dated both.

"Kinda kinky if you ask me," Cash said, "which is always a good thing, but that still doesn't help with a name."

"True." Sitting up in the bed, Wren turned thoughtful. "I had a friend at the orphanage named Priscilla.

She had the prettiest blond curls and was adopted just before her sixth birthday. Losing her was as tough as losing my dog."

"Do you have any childhood stories that aren't tear-jerkers?"

"Not so much," she admitted, "but anyway, what if we call our puppy Prissy? She's not blonde, but she does have an angelic, beauty-queen look to her that leads me to believe she'll have a great career in breaking doggy hearts."

"We talking about the same mutt?"

In a surprisingly agile move considering her size, she took the dog from him. "Come here, Precious. Don't listen to a thing he says."

"Thought you wanted to name her Prissy?"

"It's a woman's prerogative to change her mind."

Heading for the kitchen to warm the dinner Mrs. Cahwood had left them, he asked, "You're not going to pull that name-change stunt on our boy, are you?"

"Nope," she said, trailing after him with the dog riding her belly. "Especially since we're having a girl."

"YOU DO REALIZE WE HAVE a human baby due in four weeks and should be shopping for her?" In the south Tulsa Pet Warehouse, Wren peeked into her purse to find Prissy napping on the miniquilt Delores had made. "Not to mention Christmas is also barreling toward us. Have you thought about gifts?"

"Four weeks is plenty of time to get human baby gear and presents for the family." Cash grabbed a cart. "This dog baby, however, is here now and needs toys and clothes and that special food I saw advertised on TV."

"Cash, you're spoiling—ooh, look at that rhinestone collar." She made a beeline for a specialty Princess Pup endcap. Who knew there were so many adorable pooch clothes? Dresses and T-shirts and even hats and matching booties packaged in sets of four.

"Let me get this straight—if I want to buy Prissy special food, that's spoiling, but you can pick out fancy clothes when God already gave her a fur coat and that's perfectly fine?"

Wren stuck out her tongue and selected a blinged-out T-shirt that said I'm a Princess...You Scoop It!

Thirty minutes later the cart was so full with a bed and food and a plush carrying case that Wren had to ask Cash to push it to the checkout stand.

In the truck with Prissy on her lap, Wren dressed her and put on her new collar and bow.

"Know what we forgot?" Cash asked, veering the truck onto Highway 169.

"Looks like we've got everything to me." Holding up Prissy, Wren couldn't remember a time in recent history she'd ever been more content. "She's gorgeous."

"She also doesn't have a name tag. We should've at least gotten one with a phone number on it in case she gets lost or runs away."

"What number would we put? Right after the baby's born, all three of us will return to Baltimore."

Fury didn't begin to describe the sudden change in Cash's expression. Blaring the horn, he passed the car in front of them that was going five under the speed limit.

"Cash?" Wren tightened her hold on Prissy. "I've never seen you like this. What's wrong?"

"What do you think?" Cash passed another car and another.

"You know that just as soon as I'm able, the baby and I and now my puppy will all need to go home. To Baltimore. I have my residency waiting and I've even reserved a spot in the hospital's on-site day-care program. It's award winning. Our baby will receive groundbreaking infant care."

Turning on the radio, Cash flipped through stations, ultimately settling on pounding rock.

"Avoiding the issue's not going to make it go away."

"Excuse me for caring." Turning off the music, he focused on the road. "Sometimes I wish we'd never even met."

It didn't matter that he'd spoken the words out of anger—they still hurt Wren to her core. "Don't even bother going to your house. Take me straight to Tulsa International."

"Don't be ridiculous." Though they passed an exit, he didn't even slow.

Shifting on the seat, she said, "You're the one acting like a child about my leaving."

"You running away is grown-up?"

Lips pressed tight, she vowed to remain silent the rest of the way to their ranch home. Only, the place she'd once viewed as a temporary haven no longer existed. Cash had ruined it.

"Dammit, Wren, answer me. Tell me why you're still leaving. Couldn't you do your residency in Tulsa or Oklahoma City? Think about it. During the week, I can be with the baby. Isn't that better than him spending fifteen to twenty hours each day being raised by strangers?"

The last thing Wren wanted was to dignify his question with an answer, but he'd left her no choice. "Of course being with you would be better, but you're missing the point. I'm not a team player. Never have been, and I have no intention of starting now. Any time I've ever grown attached to someone or made a friend, they leave me. You'll do the same. Only instead of just me being hurt, our child will be, too. As a good mother, isn't it my job to protect my baby from pain? Especially when it inevitably stems from being abandoned by her own father?"

Shooting her a disgusted glare, he asked, "You honestly think that little of me?"

Cuddling Prissy, she snapped, "I try not to think of you at all."

"Liar."

Yes, she was. But to let him know how much his friendship had come to mean would be foolhardy. She hadn't gotten where she was today by letting people in, but by shutting them out. Remembering that was key to escaping Cash with her heart intact.

"YOU NEED TO EAT," Cash said over the chick flick he'd popped into the DVD in hopes of making Wren smile. As she no longer fit in the kitchen-table chairs, they'd taken to dining in the living room. Only, tonight she wasn't watching the movie or vacuuming her food.

"Why do you care? Remember how you wish we'd never met?" Feigning great interest in the movie, she nibbled a green bean.

"You know damn well I didn't mean that."

"Then why say it?"

"I don't know." *Probably had something to do with hurting you the way you hurt me.*

Outside, cold wind howled. Hard to believe it was already December. Where had autumn gone?

Putting her plate on the table with considerable effort, she rolled onto her side, away from the TV and him.

"Just because you can't see me doesn't mean I'm not here."

"Did I say it did?" Her voice was muffled due to her having drawn her blanket over her head.

He turned off the movie. The sudden silence was jarring, but not as much as this constant bickering.

"I was watching that" came a halfhearted complaint from somewhere under the sofa mound. Prissy peeked out from under the covers, eyeing Wren's thick-cut pork chop.

"How long do you think we have left together? Assuming the baby's on time, four weeks, and then what's a standard maternity leave? Six weeks more?"

"I've already taken too much time off. I'd like to be back in Baltimore by the first of February. As it is, I'll be lucky if the dean lets me rejoin the program midyear."

"No."

She tossed back the covers hard enough to damn near knock off the dog. "What do you mean, *no?* Last I heard you don't have a whole lot of say in the matter."

Prissy used the boost to leap onto the coffee table, helping herself to Wren's meal. Lightning fast, uncaring she'd dredged her brand-new pink shirt through ketchup, Prissy tugged the chop and herself to the table's edge, vanishing under the couch.

"Did you see that?" Cash couldn't help but laugh. "If our kid's anywhere near as sly as our dog, we've got trouble."

"No kidding." Wren also sported a slight smile.

Until their eyes met and hers filled with tears. She held out her arms and he went to her, holding her tight, praying she understood he didn't want to marry her, but he certainly didn't want her to go.

"We're going to be all right," she promised. "But this fighting has to stop. It's not good for any of us—especially my puppy, who will probably throw up all night."

Cash grinned past the knot in his throat.

Somehow, some way, bull riding was no longer his top priority. His biggest problem now? Learning to breathe without Wren and his baby and a seriously cute mutt dog.

Chapter Eleven

"How's Mommy?"

Wren cringed upon opening the door Monday morning to find Georgina carrying more fiber muffins and slung over her shoulder a bag that no doubt carried a new form of torture. "Good morning. I'm doing great. How are you?"

"Honestly," she said on her way to the kitchen, "I had my annual physical this morning, and my blood pressure is up, too. Curiously enough, when I told Doc Haven that my diet is quite healthy and I exercise every day, he suggested all of the unknowns surrounding my third grandchild might be causing me stress."

"Oh?" Ignoring Cash's mother's not-so-subtle dig, Wren helped herself to a muffin. "Thanks for bringing these. They are super-duper effective."

"You're, ah, welcome."

Catching Cash's mother off guard had become a hobby of sorts. After all, it wouldn't hurt her to at least call before her visits.

"Since needlepoint wasn't your thing, I brought you a new hobby in which I know you'll excel." When Wren returned to the sofa, head filled with remembrances of the knotted catastrophe that had occurred the last time she'd tried being crafty, Georgina pulled out a cellophane-wrapped box, brandishing the cover like a *Price Is Right* model. "Taa-daa! You're going to make a latch-hook rug to hang in the baby's room. Aren't the blue booties adorable?"

"Yes," Wren said, "but I'm pretty sure I'm having a girl."

"Nonsense." Opening the box, she drew out a large chart and a tool she pronounced to be the latch-hook instrument. "Everyone knows that if a woman craves boiled eggs during her pregnancy, she'll only give birth to boys. Mrs. Cahwood told me you've been eating dozens of her deviled eggs, which are made from boiled eggs, so there you go."

WEDNESDAY MORNING WREN found herself back in Tulsa, only this time for an ultrasound.

Constant arguing between herself and Cash had morphed into a bittersweet understanding that their remaining time together was already brief. Why poison it with petty bickering when they'd be better served preparing mentally and physically for the new life to come?

"This your first?" the ultrasound tech asked.

"Yep," Cash answered from his chair alongside Wren's padded table.

"Nervous?" the tech asked.

"Is that snow outside cold?" Again Cash acted if he was the one hauling around his thirty-pound baby!

The pretty, petite blonde laughed.

Wren suppressed the urge to smack him. Wasn't there a rule about guys who were expecting a child not flirting?

The pressure of the tech and her wand was making Wren have to pee.

"I've got a great shot of your baby's sex. Want me to print a copy for you?"

"No!" Wren snapped.

"Yes!" Cash leaned over her, trying to get a view.

"Oops." The screen had already gone blank. "Once *Mommy* told me she didn't want to see, I exited."

"Damn," Cash mumbled, shoulders slumped.

"What does it even matter?" Wren asked.

"Oh—it matters." He helped wiped the gunk off her belly, tickling in the process.

"Stop," she said with a giggle. "You know I can't stand it when you touch there."

Which only made him do it more.

"You two make a darling couple," the tech noted. "Good luck with your new family."

Wren started to correct her, but didn't.

AFTER SCRAPING SNOW FROM the truck's windows, Cash hopped into the warm cab alongside Wren. "While we're in the big city, does Prissy need anything? I noticed she's running low on Tiny T Bonz. She prefers the filet flavor over the porterhouse."

"It frightens me how you know that." She directed a heater vent toward him.

"What can I say? I take my parenting duties seriously."

"After the pet store, we really should make a stop at Baby Depot. What if she surprises us by coming early and we don't even have a crib?"

"You're right," he said, turning on the wipers and lights. "Wanna stop for lunch first? I'm seriously craving a nice, thick steak." He winked. "I'm sure our boy is, too."

After watching the mother of his child wolf down more food than he'd thought humanly possible, Cash bundled her back into the truck and headed for the baby store.

A good six inches of snow had already fallen, with no signs of a letup. Traffic was nuts, with far too many rotten drivers out on the roads.

Finally in the store's lot, Cash put the truck in Park, leaving the heater blasting. "Think I should call Mom and have her check on Prissy?"

"Probably. I would hope Mrs. Cahwood is home in front of a nice fire by now."

He dialed his mom's cell, only to five minutes later wish he hadn't. "I swear that woman's sole purpose in life is to make me miserable."

"I highly doubt that." Wren tugged on her mittens. "What'd she say?"

"Just that we need to quit playing house, pretending a puppy is our child when what we should be doing is stepping up to the real-life obligation of planning a custody visitation schedule before her blood pressure gets any higher."

"Ouch." Nibbling her lower lip, Wren asked, "Does that mean she's not checking on the puppy?"

"She'll do it, but I wouldn't be surprised if the price we pay for her services is having to hear more of her wishes and wisdom."

Once Cash had Wren safely in the store, overwhelmed didn't begin describing his avalanche of emotions. Grabbing a few things for Prissy had been fun. Selecting everything from toys to safety equipment to rectal thermometers for his child was a task he wasn't equipped to handle.

"I think I need to sit." Judging by her wide eyes, Wren wasn't faring much better.

"Want to come back when the weather's nice?"

"That's a great idea," she said, going limp from what he guessed was relief. "In the meantime, we can make a list. I'll go to some baby websites and figure out which basics we'll most need."

"Good thinking." He hustled her toward the door.

"Excuse me?" A kindly, middle-aged clerk wearing a pink-and-blue-striped Baby Depot T-shirt approached. "I couldn't help but overhear your conversation, and since I'm in charge of gift registry and have five little ones of my own, I'm fully qualified to help."

Wren was back to nibbling her lower lip.

Cash's stomach hurt.

"I, um, think we need more time." Wren hedged closer to the exit.

"Judging by the size of your baby bump," the clerk noted with a big grin, "your time is almost up."

"Could you believe that woman?" The first thing Wren did when they got home was scoop up Prissy, showering her with love. Next, she took off her heavy coat, hat and gloves before kicking off her rubber snow boots. "One would think baby-store employees would be trained to lay off the high-pressure sales tactics."

"No kidding," Cash said right behind her, scratching behind the puppy's ears.

On her way to the kitchen, Wren said, "I'm starving. Want me to make you a plate of whatever Mrs. Cahwood left?"

"Absolutely."

"On second thought…" She veered toward the bathroom. "Nature's calling."

"I knew you'd wriggle out of cooking."

"You have to admire my skill!" she shouted on her mad dash down the hall.

After washing her hands, she wound her way toward her closet to change into more comfy clothes. On such a cold night, her green fleece sweats would be extra warm.

Humming the jazzed-up version of "Rock-a-Bye Baby" that had been playing during their failed shopping mission, Wren quickly changed and then headed for the kitchen, where she hoped Cash had found something good.

Rounding the living-room corner, she found Georgina and wished she'd stayed in her room.

"Hello," Cash's mother said, rising from the sofa to give her a hug. "You look ready to pop."

"Um, thanks?"

"Have a seat," she urged, patting the sofa. "Cash tells me you two had an ultrasound this afternoon."

"Y-yes, ma'am…" Was it wrong for Wren to be terrified of what the Buckhorn matriarch might say next?

"He also said you chose to not learn the sex. I don't blame you for wanting to be surprised."

"Thank you," Wren said, relieved by Georgina's seemingly mild-mannered turn. Lowering her gaze, she laced her fingers atop the baby. "As long as he or she is healthy, I'll be happy with whatever we get."

"As long as it's a boy." Cash lit the fire and then turned to face her. Wren had always been a sucker for his smile, but something about this night's version made him extra attractive. It'd been a good day. Riding snugly alongside him in the truck while gumball-sized snow cocooned them in their own special world.

"I don't mean to be an interfering mother," Georgina said, "but Cash also told me about your failed mission to the baby store. When you two do finally get around to making a temporary nest, keep in mind that you'll want to get two of everything. One set for here, and one for Wren to take with her to Baltimore."

Though Wren was thankful the woman had finally digested the fact that she and the baby wouldn't permanently reside in Weed Gulch, something about her tone was off-putting. "Mrs. Buckhorn," Wren couldn't keep from asking, "what is it about me you don't like?"

"Excuse me?" She pressed her hand to her chest. It was a work- and weather-roughened hand with nails not painted and fancy, but filed short. "How did you draw that conclusion? I hardly even know you."

"From the day we met, I've gotten the sense that you disapprove of everything about me, from my career goals to my nonexistent craft skills to my refusal to marry your son. But one fact you need to understand is that the last thing Cash wants is to be tied down with not only a wife, but a child. Do you really want to railroad your son into a lifetime of misery out of your antiquated sense of honor?"

"Anyone up for hot chocolate?" Cash clapped his hands, smoothing them together. "Yeah, I'm thinking that's just what we need."

"Son? Is what Wren said true?" Though her eyes teared, Georgina still looked as tall and unyielding as ever.

Cash turned his back on his mother and hustled toward the kitchen. "I think Mrs. Cahwood bought me some mini-marshmallows. I'll check."

"If it is true," Georgina said, hot on his heels, "I'm sorry." The older woman's hands fluttered about her long hair, and her lips quivered.

Wren should've minded her own business, but if Cash was going to endure another attack, she felt honor bound to stand by him.

"Knowing you like I do," his mother continued, "I never thought you'd be the sort to engage in a one-night stand unless you felt an extra spark for a woman. All this time I assumed you and Wren were just playing hard to get, but would eventually realize you've fallen in love with not only each other, but your baby." Looking out the window at the still-falling snow, she added, "Again, I apologize for being a foolish old woman with ideals better suited for the last century."

At the back door Georgina took her long leather duster from a hook. After slipping it on, she removed gloves and a hat from the pockets.

"Mom..." Cash abandoned his marshmallow mission. "Don't leave like this."

"It's all right," she said. "You're an adult. Do let me know when you're having your surgery, though."

When she walked out, he chased after her. "At least let me put boots on and drive you home. You shouldn't be walking in this."

"Your father and I delivered calves out in the pasture in worse storms than this."

"Mom, please..."

Already halfway across the drive, she waved. "You two have a nice night."

Inside, with the door shut on wind and blowing snow,

Cash took off his wet socks and flung them against the stone hearth.

Again Wren followed, wishing there was something she could do to if not comfort him, at least help him calm down.

"Damn her," Cash said.

Going to Cash, she slipped her arms around his waist, wishing the baby wasn't blocking her from fully pressing against him. "I'm sorry. I don't know what got into me, confronting your mom that way. I guess that's one more thing to blame on hormones."

"Don't sweat it." He returned her hug, shielding her from whatever hurt in her world. Cash was big and strong and capable. The opposite of how she currently felt. "God's honest truth… What just happened is a huge part of why I want nothing to do with setting up my own family. I loved my dad, but as you can see, even with him gone, I still don't measure up. As great as he was, he set what, for me anyway, were unobtainable expectations."

"Did he say that? Or was it your conscience always wanting to please him?" Wren ached for Cash.

Never had she considered herself lucky for growing up not knowing her parents, but maybe there was a certain satisfaction that stemmed from having to please only herself.

Mouth dry, holding him for dear life, she said, "Did it ever occur to you that you could make a conscious decision to not be like your father? Create your own rules. Keep the parts of your upbringing you cherished, while at the same time raising our son or daughter with the qualities you wished your father had had."

"Great plan," he said with a sad laugh. "Only one problem."

"What?" Pulse racing, she prayed that problem had nothing to do with her. She'd grown to enjoy Cash's company and never wanted to hurt him.

"Practically as soon as our kid is born, you'll be taking him or her away. It's hard to implement all of these brilliant ideas when I won't even have the damned dog to practice on." He turned away from her, striding to the corner wet bar to pour a shot of Jim Beam. Downing it in one gulp, he poured another.

"That's not fair." Taking the glass from him, she dumped the amber liquid down the drain. "And getting rip-roaring drunk won't do a thing to help your emotional clarity."

Rolling his eyes, he noted, "This from our resident basket case who cries during every sappy commercial?"

"I really dislike you," she snapped.

"Ditto."

Tears started and wouldn't stop.

"Oh, come on," he said. "It's been a long day. Let's rest, and hopefully we'll wake sane in the morning."

"That's it?" He was shredding her heart, and rather than discuss it, he wanted to sleep? She longed to rail at him, but then remembered her heart had nothing to do with their situation. Per her request, they were casual friends. Yes, they'd soon share a child. Yes, Cash would forever be in her life. No, they would never share anything more.

Hand to his forehead, he sighed. "What do you want?"

"Nothing." Fighting a fresh onslaught of tears, she

woke Prissy from where she'd fallen asleep on a sofa cushion. With the dog in her arms, Wren retreated to her room.

Unfortunately, Cash followed. "Obviously you expect more of me, or you wouldn't have asked the question."

"All right…" Arms crossed, she said, "I've always heard it's not wise for a couple to go to bed angry. But since we're not a couple, in our case, that rule doesn't apply."

A muscle ticked in his jaw. "Let me get this straight—after weeks of you declaring your independence, you now all of a sudden want there to be a *you and me?*"

"No." *Yes!* But she didn't understand why. With every fiber of her being she no longer wanted to leave him. Trouble was, no matter how badly she might want to, she absolutely couldn't stay.

Chapter Twelve

"Cash?"

He woke from a deep sleep to find Wren standing alongside his bed, clutching her belly. Bolting upright, he asked, "What's wrong? Something with the baby?"

"I think so," she said, fear lacing her voice. "I woke with a horrible headache, ringing in my ears and I'm dizzy."

"Could you be getting a cold or flu?"

"I suppose, but all of those are signs of high blood pressure." Wringing her hands, she looked lost. "I've been meaning to get a home pressure monitor, but they're expensive and I felt funny asking you for money when the last time we were at the drugstore I felt fine."

"Are you kidding me?" Out of bed, he rummaged through his dresser for a clean T-shirt and socks. Finding yesterday's jeans where he'd left them over the end of his footboard, he pulled them on over his boxers. "What's wrong with you? You didn't mind me spending a small fortune on new clothes for your dog, but when it came to watching your own health, pride got in the way?"

"It wasn't like that," she said.

He snorted. "You already call Doc Haven?"

"Uh-huh. He said with the weather, it'd be fastest for you to drive me into Tulsa. He's called ahead to Saint Francis hospital, so they'll be expecting us."

"What're they going to do?" he asked as he headed for her room, where he found her a giant sweatshirt to slip on over her flannel nightgown.

Miraculously, she didn't fight him about his choice, instead lifting her arms for him to help put it on. "I would imagine order a twenty-four-hour urine test for protein. Put me on a fetal monitor to test the baby's heart rate and to see if he or she is feeling any stress."

"Less chitchat, more action." Nudging her toward the front door, he asked, "Need anything else?"

"What about Prissy? She's too tiny to stay here alone." Wren was so unsteady on her feet that Cash had to reach out a couple of times to steady her.

"Your mutt will be fine," he assured her. "In the morning I'll call Mrs. Cahwood and ask her to take the dog home with her until we get back."

"Thank you," she said, standing on her tiptoes to kiss his cheek. "This is scary enough together. I can't fathom going it alone."

He wished for an elegant turn of phrase to comfort her, but he was fresh out of poetry. "Wait here," he said after pulling on her coat, hat and mittens. "I'll be right back with the truck. And while you wait," he called halfway out the door as an afterthought, "sit."

Thirty minutes later Cash barreled down the Turner Turnpike as fast as crappy road conditions allowed. One lane had been plowed, but no way was he able to go his usual seventy-five.

Wren intermittently dozed, and if it hadn't been for her seat belt holding her upright, he was fairly certain she'd have long since slumped onto his lap.

What had her sweet kiss been about? Why did he care? It bugged him that in such a short time she'd become his everything. Before her arrival he'd fixated on nothing but his knee. Calculating over and over the time until he rejoined the tour. Now he had fleeting moments when he wasn't so sure he even wanted to go back out on the road. As much fun as he had playing with Wren's pup, he couldn't fathom what holding his son for the first time would do to his heart.

Piggyback rides and sledding and building snowmen and forts in the winter. In the summer he'd sign him up for Little League and 4-H—all the things his father had done with him. All four Buckhorn men and Daisy would fish and hike and sit around campfires soaking in stories of how their great-grandfather and Duke had pieced their land together like a patchwork quilt. Buying parcels here and there until he'd made it into the powerhouse it was today.

Dallas and Wyatt oversaw the farming and running cattle. Breeding top-notch quarter horses and even pumping oil. It was a huge undertaking keeping all their father's endeavors in good order. His mom worked too hard. As did his brothers. None of them seemed to resent his spending nearly every weekend on the road, but secretly, did they?

Wren stirred. "Where are we?"

"Just east of Sapulpa. Won't be long now." The snow had stopped and this part of the state hadn't been hit nearly as hard as the ranch. "While you're up, I've been meaning to ask what kind of trouble high blood pressure can cause. I mean, you hear about it with older folks, but I never thought of it as being a problem for pregnant women."

She yawned and rubbed her eyes. "As a formal diagnosis, it's called preeclampsia. The main concern is in causing narrowing of blood vessels, including the ones in the placenta and umbilical cord. This leads to the baby not getting enough oxygen or nutrients." Drawing a snowflake on the fogged window, she added, "If left untreated, it can lead to placental abruption, seizures, premature birth, coma."

"Swell." Instinctively he reached for her hand, easing his fingers between hers. "But that's not going to happen to us, right? Because we're treating you and the baby in time?"

"Right." Taken at face value, her answer was positive enough, but knowing her as he did, he knew she couldn't hide her lingering fear. He recognized it in the dampness of her palm. The way her expression had glazed—as if she hadn't shared the full extent of her worries.

How long until she trusted him completely? Would the time ever come? Considering how standoffish he'd been in regard to their one day being a couple, did he deserve having her rely on him? Not only for her and their child's financial support, but emotionally?

"You gave me quite a scare," Doc Haven said to Wren in her hospital room the next morning. She and the baby were hooked up to so many monitors she felt more like a robot than soon-to-be mom. "Thought you'd been taking it easy so this wouldn't happen?"

"I was, but Cash and I got into a tiff and I guess things went downhill from there."

"Your vitals look good for the moment. Blood pressure's higher than I'd like, but I've seen worse and still delivered plenty of healthy babies. Once I've got your urine results, we'll reassess."

Nodding, she said, "Thanks. This is the first time I've seen a hospital from this perspective, and it's scary. I much prefer being the doctor to the patient." The newly remodeled maternity wing featured wood laminate flooring and soothing floral wallpaper. There was an oak rocker, built-in sofa and even a recliner. Botanical prints and striped curtains finished what designers had hoped to be a warm, friendly birthing environment. A thoughtful nurse or aide had even hung red and silver garlands for the holidays. If it weren't for the monitors, Wren could almost have imagined herself in a hotel.

Chuckling, the white-haired man made a few notations on her chart, then promised to release her as soon as he felt it was safe for her and the baby.

WREN HAD FINALLY MANAGED to drift off to sleep when Cash bumped open the door and entered the room.

"Everything okay?" Carrying three bags of chips, a microwave burrito and two Cokes, Cash said, "I ran into Doc Haven in the hall."

"Our baby's fine. Me, too," Wren assured him. With the exception of the butterflies winging through her stomach every time she saw her baby's father, she thought. He'd been so good to her. The whole night, never leaving her side. His jawline sported dusky brown stubble and his longish curls looked as if they'd developed a halo. Wren knew the effect was caused by perpetual hat head, but she'd grown to like it all the same. Then there were his eyes. Darker this morning— like the perfect Christmas tree she'd wanted to hike through the woods to find.

"Did the doc say when you're getting sprung?" Upon settling into the recliner, he carefully arranged his snacks on Wren's nightstand.

"Probably tomorrow. And FYI, the smell of that burrito is *no bueno*."

Poised with the offensive thing at his mouth, he asked, "Want me to eat it out in the waiting area?"

"No. I could probably still smell it from there."

He downed it in three bites. "Did I do anything in particular to tick you off—besides eating?"

"Sorry. I'm antsy." Hands folded on top of her belly, Wren sighed. "Throughout my pregnancy I guess I've played this game in my head that it wasn't really happening. Sounds nuts, but it was a way to cope. I'm afraid of everything. How I'm going to do justice to both being a parent and completing my residency." Covering her face with her hands, she was even afraid of crying again.

"Time out." Cash abandoned his food to draw down her hands, easing his fingers between hers. "For the moment, how about we tackle one problem at a time, which is getting you out of here and back home."

She nodded, holding on to him for dear life.

"After that, you and I are going to sit down and come up with a list of kid gear. If we managed to get a puppy through her first weeks at home, being two reasonably intelligent adults, we can do the same for our child."

"You think?" At the moment she didn't feel capable of walking to the bathroom on her own. Weak and trembling and bigger than three houses, Wren was shocked by how rapidly her hard-won independence had faded. Had she ever truly been in control of her life, or had that control been an illusion?

"Honey, I remember when my sister-in-law was close to delivering Betsy and Bonnie and trust me, she was nutty as a Christmas fruitcake. Crying constantly, and when she wasn't sporting tears, she'd snap like a pit bull. It wasn't a good time. I can't imagine what you're going through, but you have to get it through that thick head of yours that no matter what, I'm here for you."

"But you shouldn't be," she argued, crying anew. "You need surgery right away so you can rejoin your tour."

"What I need..." He released one of her hands to tuck flyaway strands of her hair behind her ears. "Is for you to understand my bull riding is on the back burner. Even if my knee were a hundred percent, I wouldn't leave you or our baby in this condition. Now, take some deep breaths and focus on nothing but getting our baby safely into our arms."

"Surprise!"

Hands to her chest, Wren felt her legs nearly go out from under her in the doorway of Cash's home as she saw every person she knew in Weed Gulch smiling and clapping in welcome. Delores and Doc Haven. Sally, Doc's nurse. Georgina and Stella. Dallas and the twins and Cash's brother, Wyatt. Mrs. Cahwood—even Henry, the ranch foreman, whom Wren had met only twice. After two days in her quiet hospital room, the noisy show of affection brought on instant tears.

Someone flipped a switch, immersing the room in

an incredible holiday glow. Tiny white lights had been strung in a fragrant pine. Glittering ornaments had been hung from each bough. Beneath the tree were presents. Dozens—maybe even a hundred. Every inch of the house had been decked out in Christmas cheer, from the three stockings hanging from the mantel to fresh pine garlands strung over each door. The scents of evergreen and cinnamon and freshly baked gingerbread completed the holiday wonderland.

Georgina stepped forward, crushing Wren in an unexpected hug. "You gave us a scare. I'm so glad you're feeling better. We all are."

"Thank you. It's good to be home."

When Cash entered, his brothers and friends drew him aside for plenty of laughter and backslapping.

Georgina drew Wren a short way down the hall. "Before your baby shower really gets under way, I owe you another apology. I'm sorry we got off on the wrong foot. *Really.* Chalk it up to an old woman's insecurities. I hate that it took you being in the hospital to force me to my senses, but that's the truth. I thought by sheer stubborn will I could make you and my son fall in love, but if it's not meant to be, then so be it. I can't live with this animosity between us. Whether you're here or in Baltimore, I'd very much like to be part of my grandchild's life."

"Of course," Wren said. "A baby can never have too much love. I'm sorry, too." And Wren truly was. There had been times she could've taken the higher ground and backed away from their confrontations, but hadn't.

Taking Wren by the arm, Cash's mother helped her off with her outer garments before guiding her to a comfortable armchair. The twins pushed an ottoman beneath Wren's swollen feet.

Delores leaned in, giving Wren's shoulder a squeeze. "A little birdie told us you and Cash are behind on baby shopping."

"That's an understatement." Wren shared a smile with her friend, realizing that in the short time she'd lived in Weed Gulch, she'd met people she never wanted to let go. For the first time in her life, she felt part of something bigger than herself. As if she was a better person for knowing everyone in the room.

With Prissy squirming in her arms, Bonnie asked, "Do we have to wait for *all* of those presents to open before we get cake?"

Everyone laughed.

Dallas ruffled his daughter's hair. "This is Wren and your uncle Cash's party. You'll have to ask them."

Cash deferred to Wren, pouring on his ample charm with a lopsided grin that left her feeling drunk on happiness. "Ma'am?"

"Tell you what," she said, tweaking Bonnie's nose and then the puppy's, "if you promise to bring me a big piece, then I say you should have all the cake you want."

With their guests retreating to the kitchen, Cash sat on the arm of her chair. "Having fun?"

Unable to speak past the knot in her throat, she nodded.

"Me, too."

"I—I'm assuming you planned all of this?"

He shrugged. "I had a lot of help from the ladies in my life. While Betsy and Bonnie took their dad to the bakery for the perfect cake, Mom, Stella and Delores went on a baby gear roundup." After kissing her forehead, he leaned back, allowing their gazes to lock. Their connection was dizzying. The equivalent of six glasses of champagne.

"What's happening?" she whispered.

"I'm no expert," he said, close enough to her lips for his warm breath to tickle, "but if I'm lucky, I'm getting the strangest suspicion Mommy may be falling for Daddy."

Chapter Thirteen

"If those people were truly our friends," Cash said the next day from the floor of Wren's bedroom with Prissy looking on, "they would've stuck around to help put this stuff together."

Wren didn't look up from the crib assembly manual she was reading.

"Are you even listening?" he complained.

"What?" She looked up, in the process releasing a cascade of her long dark hair over her shoulder. He'd always considered her a beauty, but the way she sat in a pool of bright winter sun made her skin glow. If they had a baby girl, would she be as pretty as her mom?

"Last night," Cash said, pulse racing faster than it had conquering his toughest bull, "I said something that I no doubt shouldn't have, but…" He cleared his throat. "I—I need to know if what I was feeling was just an issue of circumstance—you know, both of us wrapped up in the festive mood—or more?"

"I can't do this," she said, sharply looking away.

"Can't do what? Answer my question? Take a chance on me? *Us?*"

Sighing, she tried standing, but ended up looking like an upside-down ladybug.

Prissy barked, thinking it was time to play.

"Need help?" Crouching behind her, he hefted her onto her feet. The motion hurt his knee, but that didn't bother him nearly as much as Wren's refusal to talk about issues that mattered.

"I'm tired. Would you mind if we finish later?"

"Take your mutt and nap in my bed," he suggested. "Unless you want our baby sleeping in a dresser drawer, this needs to get done."

"Please don't be angry. I heard you—I just don't know what to say. Truth? I felt the same. Like in that moment everything we'd ever dared dream of might be coming true. But they're called dreams for a reason, Cash. Because for the vast majority of people, they only occur deep in people's minds in the black of night. They aren't real."

Slamming down his screwdriver, Cash used every ounce of control not to punch the wall. "On the flip side," he pointed out, "my parents were very happily married for thirty-eight years. Dallas and Bobbie Jo are another classic case of love conquering all."

Making her escape, she called over her shoulder, "Sure, Cash, let's talk about how great those relationships turned out for both your mom and brother. Your dad and Bobbie Jo are dead. Dead, Cash."

He followed her out into the hall. "Despite that, I know for a fact that had Mom and Dallas known in advance their spouses would die too young they would've married anyway."

Spinning to face him, she said, "You're not even making sense. You've told me a half dozen times you want nothing to do with marriage."

"I know, but what was it you told me not too long ago about having the prerogative to change your mind?"

She opened her mouth, only to cover it with her hands. Turning from him, she walked straight to the freezer and grabbed for her Chunky Monkey ice cream.

Prissy sat at her feet, begging.

After getting a spoon, Wren scooped a small portion into the dog's crystal bowl, then ate her own straight from the container.

Cash pushed himself up to sit on the granite counter. "All the ice cream in the world isn't going to change things between us. Your advice on me remembering my father and upbringing but raising our kid with my own style—it made sense. Seeing you in the hospital, realizing how much having you in my life means..." Hopping off the counter, he took the ice cream and spoon from her, setting them on the table before cupping her face with his hands. "Marry me, Wren, not because my mother and the entire town think it's the right thing to do, but because you'll die without having a cowboy stud like me permanently entrenched in your life."

"But we hardly know each other. There's my residency and..."

Tracing the delicate arch of her eyebrows, all the while never dropping her stare, he dared her to deny him. "I was really touched by my family and friends coming together for us last night. It made me see that maybe beyond my fear of not being a good father or husband was an extra-large helping of Buckhorn pride. For as long as I can remember I've done the opposite of what people expected or wanted me to do, sometimes for no good reason other than being ornery. In our case,

I now realize that in letting you and our baby go, I'd only be spiting myself."

"How?" she fairly squeaked. "How do you know? Is it a feeling deep inside or a voice? I'm so afraid if I allow myself to fall for you, I'll never be independent again. I'll never complete my residency or earn my medical license. I'll become a lonely drifter like most of the kids I grew up with. Can't you understand?"

He traced her lips. Full, lovely, kissable lips he was finished even trying to resist.

Pressing his mouth to hers earned him the sweetest mew. She leaned fully into him, clinging to his shirt with the kind of openmouthed hunger he'd craved ever since their wild Vegas night.

"Marry me," he demanded rather than asked.

"Okay," she said, kissing him again as if he were her air. "But if we go bad, don't say I didn't warn you."

"OVER THE TOP?" STELLA asked three days later.

Not wishing to hurt the woman's feelings, Wren wasn't sure how to reply. They sat in the duck-themed living room of Marva Wells, who was apparently the master baker for all of Tohwalla county. With the wedding scheduled for Saturday, Georgina was back home with the florist, making hasty plans for every inch of the main house to be decked out in Christmas finery.

Sandwiched between Stella and Cash, Wren perched on the sofa with Marva's portfolio balanced on her knees. The current page showed a six-tiered wedding cake complete with a fountain and glittering swan topper that was magnificent, but more fitting for royalty than a sweet ceremony intended for family and a few close friends.

"Um." Wren struggled to form a thought past how amazing Cash's leathery aftershave smelled. Never would she have predicted her life would turn out this way, but now that it had, she abandoned herself to the giddy, girlie pleasure of planning their special day.

"Maybe something smaller would be more appropriate."

"I disagree," Cash said, all too pleasantly pressing against her as he reached for one of the sample cake pieces Marva had placed on her coffee table. Ignoring the plastic fork, he dredged his finger through the frosting. "Mmm...good." Repeating the motion, he offered the same sugary treat to Wren.

Momentarily forgetting the other two people in the room, she licked and sucked his finger clean. When their eyes met, there was no denying the heat she'd long suppressed.

Stella gave Cash a swat. "I'm glad your mama's not here, or she'd tan your hide for such a public display."

Wren's cheeks flamed from the remembrance of every bare inch of Cash's splendid *hide*. Was it wrong for her to now be as happy as she'd once been confused?

"It's quite all right," Marva assured her. "Just last week I worked with a drunken groom who requested beer-flavored frosting."

Stella blanched.

Cash grinned. "Damn. Why didn't I think of that?"

Wren rolled her eyes. "Consider yourself booted from the cake committee."

Talking to Wren's belly, he complained, "Can you believe the way your mother treats me? We're not even married and already she's bossing me around."

"Ignore him," Stella urged. "We have to make this decision ASAP, as we still have a dress to find."

"Give me that book," Cash said, and flipped rapid-fire through the pages. After twenty or so, he pointed to a dreamy quadruple-tiered confection. Since the tiers were small, it had the feel of a classical wedding cake without being overdone. The bottom layer was square with diamond-patterned piping. The next layer was round with wide fondant stripes, followed by another square layer with lacy piping. At the top was a tiny round cake dotted with sugar pearls and a white bouquet of sugar roses. Each layer was ringed with more sugar pearls and roses. "This work for you?"

Tossing her arms around his neck, she answered with a kiss.

Clearing her throat, Stella said, "Marva, it seems we've made a decision."

The cake lady laughed. "That was the easy part. Now you have to select the flavors and fillings."

"I DON'T KNOW ABOUT THIS, man." If Dallas scowled any harder, Cash was pretty sure his face would forever freeze that way. "Mom's gonna eat you alive for not picking a more conservative suit."

Surveying himself in the dressing-room mirror of the Woodland Hills Mall Dillard's, Cash couldn't help but grin at his own reflection. "Damn, I'm good-looking."

Arms folded, Dallas tapped the toe of his boot. "Time's ticking, bro."

"And? I'm done."

"This is a mistake," Dallas said. "Weddings should

be solemn occasions. As such, you should dress the part."

"Tell you what." Cash took off his jacket. "If I ever marry you, I'll be sure to keep that in mind."

Twenty minutes later they stopped off at the food court before the long ride home.

Dallas had salad with low-fat dressing.

Cash had Frito chili pie.

Joining Dallas at a table in the seating area, Cash dug in.

"How did all of this come about?" Dallas asked, still fussing with his napkin on his lap.

"What? The wedding?"

Big brother nodded. "Last I heard you and Wren were dead set against marital bliss."

"We were. To a certain extent we still are. But the whole hospital thing gave us a hellacious scare. For me, anyway, it got me thinking about my priorities. It pains me to admit it, but you were right. No matter what, family comes first. Before Wren, my next bull ride was my world. Now…" Choked up, he looked away and smiled.

"I'm happy for you." Holding his hand across the table, Dallas grasped Cash's hand. "Welcome to adulthood. It's been a long time coming."

"Happy?" Georgina asked Wren during a lull in the rehearsal dinner conversation. The Buckhorn main house had been transformed into a Christmas wedding wonderland—white and purple poinsettias, pine garlands and plenty of sparkling lights, candles and silver ornament accents.

"Aside from constant heartburn, a tiny elbow between my ribs and swollen feet, I'm floating on clouds."

Cash's mother laughed. "Ah, I remember those days well. At least it's almost over."

"True."

The meal had been a decadent blend of steak and lobster tails, twice-baked potatoes and pencil-thin asparagus dripping in butter and Parmesan cheese. Cheesecake, coffee and herbal tea had provided the perfect end to an enchanted evening.

The guys were engrossed in talk of football play-offs, and Stella had taken the twins off to bed. Delores had gone home early, leaving Wren and her soon-to-be mother-in-law on their own.

Georgina said, "You had me convinced that this wedding wasn't in your cards."

Grimacing, Wren admitted, "I didn't think it was. Even though Cash and I connected the second we met, I refused to believe it possible to merge a husband and baby with my medical career."

"Will you be completing your residency in Tulsa?"

"Most likely." Taking a roll from a basket, she daubed on butter. "I've started the transfer process with my dean, but there's a lot of paperwork involved. This late in the year, I might have to start over in July, but we'll see. Winning my Baltimore residency was quite a coup. Only ten out of two thousand applicants were accepted."

"Wow…"

Wren forced a breath. Caught up in the wedding excitement, she'd forgotten what an honor she'd been given.

"Please don't take this the wrong way," her future

mother-in-law said, "but I had no idea you were so accomplished. I can only imagine what a shock your pregnancy must've been."

No kidding.

Mouth dry, Wren struggled with a moment of panic over her recent hasty moves. Then she looked to Cash. He met her gaze and they shared a smile. Calm flooded through her. In marrying him, she was making the right decision. For her baby and for herself.

"I found out I was carrying Dallas at a point when his father was constantly on the road working for an oil exploration company. The thought of raising him without Duke was almost more than I could bear, but the time flew by and I actually missed some aspects of being solely in charge."

"How did you reconcile your professional needs with those of your family?"

Turning introspective, Georgina folded her cloth napkin. "When Duke and I were married, women didn't really have careers. Sure, there were nurses and secretaries and schoolteachers, but I'd never even met a female doctor or dentist until I was in my fifties."

Which was yet another facet of why continuing her career meant so much to Wren. She'd always had an innate need to prove herself. Being married wouldn't make that go away.

"Did you know Mrs. Cahwood was a Rockette?"

"Did I know? I begged my parents to let me go with her. She was the exception to the Weed Gulch rule that women belonged in the home. When Yvette danced, you just knew she was destined for more. I was heartbroken when she gave up New York City to return home, but she's told me on numerous occasions that she never regretted her decision."

"Did you?" Wren was almost afraid to ask, but she was enjoying getting to know Cash's mom as a woman rather than his parent, and she genuinely wanted to know.

"You mean did I resent giving up any dreams I might've had to support Duke in achieving his?" Again her expression seemed far-off. As if she'd become so comfortable in her current role as matriarch that it required a trip back in time to touch base with the woman she'd once been. "In retrospect, no. I've led an amazingly blessed life. But I'd be lying if I told you Duke and I didn't suffer our share of growing pains. Once the boys and their sister were all in school, I wanted to take a floral-design class in the hopes of being hired by the florist in the next town over. Well, once Duke heard the class met during the day and that I would need his help with laundry and the meals and such, he flat-out refused. Said he'd rather spend the money on buying me new dresses. For months I resented him."

"What happened?" Leaning forward, Wren asked, "Did you ever take the class?"

"Years later, on my fortieth birthday, Duke surprised me with fully paid tuition. As well as an apology for taking such a hard-line stance the first time around."

"Did you ever land a job in floral design?"

"I did." Laughing, she said, "It was right around Easter and turns out I was deathly allergic to lilies. I lasted all of a week until I was missing volunteering at the kids' school and my weekly bridge games and church meetings. Still, it meant the world to me that Duke finally came around to encouraging me to try following my own dreams. One thing about Cash is that I believe he'll wholeheartedly support you in whatever course you decide is right for you."

Placing her hand over Georgina's, Wren confessed, "If I didn't believe that, we wouldn't be having a wedding tomorrow night."

Chapter Fourteen

"In all of the excitement," Cash said on the short walk home, "I forgot to mention how amazing you look in that blue sweater."

"Thanks." Wren snuggled against him to ward off the crisp December chill. Though the brick-paved road had long since been cleared, snow still covered much of the rolling prairie. Reflected moonlight illuminated their every step. "For the record, it's aquamarine. You're looking quite dapper in pomegranate."

"Do you have any idea how hard my rodeo buddies would laugh at me for having the words *aquamarine* or *pomegranate* in my vocabulary?"

"From what I've heard," she teased, "*real* men aren't afraid of color."

Cash used her dig as his invitation to tickle.

He loved Wren's laugh. Her shrieking giggles were the stuff dreams were made of. She all too soon begged him to stop or she'd wet her pants. Knowing how much she'd peed of late, he knew she wasn't kidding. He also knew how much he wanted to kiss her.

Hugging her to him, he pressed his lips to her forehead, her nose, her lips. Her soft, pliable delicious lips that no matter how many times he sampled, he never tired of tasting.

"Mmm…" She clung to him, moaning for more, which he was only too happy to give. Pressed against him as she was, Cash had a tough time remembering to be a gentleman. He hadn't dreamed it possible, but her breasts had grown even larger and felt incredibly hot in his palms.

Their kiss deepened to the point his head was swimming from the rush of blood servicing his erection. "I want you so bad."

"I know," she said, panting breaths clouding the frigid night air. "We were so busy arguing at my last doctor appointment, we forgot to ask permission."

"Doesn't matter," he said, his forehead against hers. "At this stage, I probably shouldn't be fooling around down there."

Giggling, kissing, she asked, "*Down there?* What are you, twelve?"

"Judging by my current frustration level, that's about how old I feel. At least I got some boob action."

"You're incorrigible," she playfully scolded.

"And damned good-looking."

"Goes without saying."

"And for the record," he added, "back to your antiquated definition of *real* men, honey, I'm as real as it gets and I am afraid of my very pregnant almost-wife catching a chill. Want me to carry you the rest of the way?"

"Does my waddle embarrass you?"

"Not a bit. But your chattering teeth I find most alarming." Almost to the house, he asked, "You and

Mom seemed to be engrossed in something. She wasn't complaining about me, was she?"

"To the contrary, much of the conversation centered around her life, but she did add what a great man you've become."

"Really?" Eyebrows raised, Cash had a tough time believing his mom didn't view him as a total screwup. Especially now that his knee was so wrecked he might never ride again.

"You seem surprised."

"I am. As the youngest of our clan, I've spent my life in everyone else's shadow. Wyatt has a fancy business degree he uses to help Dallas with the ranch. Dallas's degree is in animal husbandry—like what does that even mean? My sister's raking in big bucks with her law degree. Then there's you. You'll have a string of credentials after your name, half of which I won't even understand."

"If you want a PhD, sweetheart, then go to school. It's not that big of a deal."

Inside, Cash helped her off with her winter gear.

While she changed into her pj's and slippers, he started a fire. He was getting married the next day to a woman he couldn't get enough of, so why was he all of a sudden feeling blue?

Staring into the flames, he lost himself in fears.

What happened if his surgery didn't work and he was kicked off the tour? Yes, he had more cash than he knew what to do with in savings, but that wasn't going to last forever. Would Wren eventually think him less of a man for not sharing her education level?

"What's wrong?" she asked, in her fleece looking

like a fluffy bunny he wanted to hold on his lap and stroke.

"Nothing." Forcing a smile, he motioned her to join him on the hearth.

"No one has a pout quite like you, Cash Buckhorn. Out with it." She tried sitting beside him, but didn't fit. "Guess it's the sofa for me."

"At dinner, my brothers spouted statistics about how marriages where one spouse has a degree and the other doesn't typically end in divorce. I don't want us to end up as a statistic."

Shaking her head, she sighed. "You, dear, have too much time on your hands. Mark my words, once the baby's here and you're back into your training you'll feel more like your own self."

"Promise?"

"Wish I could," she said with genuine concern. "But that would be like you reassuring me my residency transfer will magically go through. In marrying, we're both assuming a certain amount of risks."

Though he hated asking, he couldn't stop. "For you, are those risks worth it? Playing devil's advocate, if your transfer doesn't get approved, will you resent me?"

Her flicker of indecision told him more than he'd ever cared to know.

"YOU'RE A BEAUTIFUL BRIDE," Mrs. Cahwood gushed while easing rhinestone pins into Wren's hair. To accommodate her lacy veil, the front was swept away from her face, while the back was a cascade of curls.

"Thank you." Wren hadn't thought it possible to find a maternity wedding gown that made her feel like a princess, but she should've known better than to underestimate the power Georgina had in moving mountains to get her way. After selecting her dream satin gown in a Tulsa bridal shop, it had then been rush altered to fit. With a full, tulle-lined skirt, sweetheart neckline, miles of white satin and enough seed pearls and crystals for her to blind airline pilots were she to stand in the sun, Wren hoped her groom found her as beautiful as she felt.

Prissy, snoozing on the bed, wore a specially made rhinestoned doggy dress for the occasion.

"Nervous?" her friend asked, standing back to appraise her work.

"Funny, but no. It's almost as if my entire life has led me to this moment." She did, however, have a slight stomachache. Almost like period cramps, but considering her current state, that was unlikely.

"Good." The housekeeper squeezed her in a hug. "There are, however, a few items we're missing. For something old, I thought you might do me the honor of wearing these…." Eyes shining, she took a Tiffany box from her purse, opening it to reveal spellbinding diamond cascade earrings.

Wren gasped.

"Impressive, huh?" Helping Wren put them on, she said, "They were an opening-night gift from a Wall Street tycoon named Geoffrey Bartholomew Wentworth IV. He wanted me to marry him in the worst way, but I just kept telling him I couldn't be bothered with wifely duties." She winked. "I'd been born to dance. I've kept them all these years as not only a keepsake, but a nest egg. Now I want you to have them."

"I couldn't," Wren insisted. "They're too valuable."

Mrs. Cahwood waved off Wren's objections. "Making

you smile is far more valuable. Please, I want to know that even after I'm gone, they'll still be treasured."

Hugging her friend, Wren said, "I love you." And she meant it.

A knock sounded at the guest room's door. In popped two matching girls, followed by their grandmother and nanny.

"Lovely," Georgina said, catching her first glimpse of the bride. "Cash is going to be blown away."

"I hope so," Wren admitted.

"Yvette," Stella said, "those earrings of yours are even prettier than I remember. Why didn't you bring them out at my wedding?"

"You never asked," the former dancer teased.

"Since I see you're already wearing your something old," Cash's mom said, "we still need borrowed, blue and new." Nudging her granddaughters, she said, "Ladies, do you have something for your new aunt?"

Bonnie held out an exquisite pearl-and-diamond bracelet. Her expression very serious for a five-year-old, she said, "If you don't like this, I'll wear it."

"Thank you," Wren said, touched beyond words by not only the bracelet's beauty, but the love that had gone into selecting such a perfect piece. "I can't begin to describe how much all of this means."

"You don't have to," Stella said, brushing tears from Wren's flawless makeup. "It's written all over your face." Stepping back, she put her index finger to her lips. "You're looking pretty darned good, but there are still a couple of things missing. Betsy, hon, it's your turn."

With much pomp and ceremony in her fancy long satin dress, Betsy held up a lacy handkerchief that had been meticulously embroidered with bluebonnets and ivy. Scrunching her face as if trying to remember a speech, Betsy said, "This is really, super-duper old and I forget who used it, but there aren't any boogers."

Georgina gasped. "Betsy Buckhorn, after practicing all morning, that was the best you could do?"

"Sorry, Grandma, but I'm awfully hungry and hafta make a pee-pee."

Laughing, Wren said, "You did perfect, and I'm sure your grandmother can fill me in on the details."

"'Kay." Crossing her legs and doing the potty dance, Betsy asked, "Can I go now?"

While her twin scampered off without permission, Bonnie shook her head. "She's so childish."

"For the record," Georgina said, "that handkerchief was made by my Irish great-great-great-grandmother Kate and has been carried in every wedding in my family line since."

Tears stung the back of Wren's eyes and her throat felt in danger of forever knotting. Her stomachache was now working overtime. Regardless, she was determined to enjoy this magical afternoon and night. "You all are the best. Thank you doesn't seem adequate."

"It's perfect," Stella said while fussing with more makeup repair. "So where does that leave us?"

"Borrowed," Georgina said, stepping forward with Wren's final gift. "On the surface, this may seem ridiculous, but Cash's father won this for me on our first official date at the Tulsa State Fair. Now, to an Oklahoman, it's still a big event, but all those years ago it might as well have been Christmas, Easter and Thanksgiving all rolled into one."

"Amen," Stella said with a firm nod.

Mrs. Cahwood yawned. "Frankly, I always found the whole thing overrated."

The comment earned her swats from both of her contemporaries.

"As I was saying," Cash's mother continued, with her object still hidden, "Duke won this for me and I believe it's brought me luck ever since." Opening her hand, she revealed the ugliest, ragtag Kewpie doll ever on God's green earth. It wasn't much over two inches tall, but the hair was orange, body naked and eyes a little spooky with glowing red stones. "Isn't he the cutest thing ever? I'll tuck him in your bouquet and no one will ever see him."

"Grandma," Bonnie said, hiding behind Wren's train, "that thing's scary. Put it away."

Though she'd never let on to her future mother-in-law, Wren couldn't have agreed more.

WATCHING HIS BRIDE DESCEND the staircase he'd sledded down as a little boy, Cash felt ready to bust with pride. The closer Wren came, the more he wanted the ceremony over and the honeymoon to begin—not that they were headed anywhere. Doc Haven had ordered her straight to bed after all the excitement. Still, Cash couldn't wait to finally, officially have her all to himself.

His mother had hired a local band to play for the ceremony and reception. "Here Comes the Bride" had never sounded sweeter than with acoustic guitars and a few fiddles.

Bonnie and Betsy made adorable flower girls. Granted, some of the red rose petals hit the walls and guests like projectiles, but at least the girls looked good while acting like the hellions they usually were.

Wren was next down the temporary aisle. Stella and his mother had found a good fifty woven willow chairs, softened by Santa-themed cushions. Candles and holly and the rich scent of pine had transformed his family home into a Christmas wedding wonderland.

Despite all of his mom and Stella's work, the most exquisite part of the ceremony was his bride. "You take my breath away," he said when she reached him.

"You're not looking too shabby yourself." Her hands lightly trembled, but the light in her smiling eyes told him all he needed to know. "I'm loving your derriere in those blue jeans."

He tipped his black cowboy hat. "Dallas thought you wouldn't, but I knew damn well you would."

The preacher performing the service cleared his throat. "Whenever you two are ready, we'll begin."

Most weddings Cash had attended were dignified and brimming with deep meaning. His was a seriously good time with both the groom and the bride making plenty of mix-ups and flirty double entendres until at long last reaching the most important part.

Reverend Winthrop seemed grateful to wrap things up. "I now—thank heavens—pronounce you husband and wife. Cash Buckhorn, you may kiss your bride."

Whoops and hollers from all in attendance prefaced a kiss that rocketed through Cash with enough force to make him weak in his knees.

"Mrs. Buckhorn," he whispered in his wife's ear on their walk down the aisle, "what are you getting me for Christmas now that I have everything I've ever wanted?"

Wren grimaced in pain then stopped to clutch her belly. "W-will a son or daughter work?"

Chapter Fifteen

On their own for the brief time it took their guests to rise from their seats, Cash asked Wren, "Do I need to get you to a hospital?"

"No," Wren said, wincing through a smile. "I want to enjoy our reception. I've had a few contractions today, but I'm pretty sure they're just Braxton Hicks."

"In English for the nondoctors in the crowd."

"Practice contractions. Unless they become regular, we have nothing to worry about."

"Are you sure?" Cupping her cheek, he searched her eyes. Did he think she'd lie about something like this?

"Sweetie, of course I'm sure. I may be a disaster when it comes to shopping for baby gear, but on the medical side, I've got it—" ouch "—under control."

The rest of the night passed in a pleasantly painful blur. The Braxton Hicks continued, but Wren was having too much fun to worry about the timing.

The band was amazing, mixing romantic slow songs with plenty of rowdy country tunes. Though she didn't know the vast majority of guests, the longtime family friends and neighbors proved to be great partiers.

Taking a breather in the kitchen, she found Georgina

directing a caterer on adding more sherbet to the punch.

"I can't thank you enough," Wren said, pulling her aside. "This night will forever top my favorite memories."

"I'm glad you enjoyed it." Turning her head to swipe tears, Georgina excused herself to find a tissue.

"What's wrong?" Wren asked her mother-in-law.

"Has Cash told you much about his sister, Daisy?"

"No." Silently bearing another contraction, Wren took a second to catch her breath. "Just that she lives in San Francisco and you don't see her as much as you'd like."

"I understand she's busy, and we're all proud of her for earning her law degree, but for the life of me I can't fathom what could keep her away from something as important as her baby brother's wedding."

"I'm sorry." Wren took her hand. "I'm sure whatever Daisy's doing, you're on her mind."

Hugging Wren, Georgina said, "I'm so happy to have you as my daughter. Even better, as my friend—although that may be on a probationary status if I don't get a decent craft out of you."

"SURE YOU'RE ALL RIGHT?" Helping himself to thirds of the cake he'd selected, Cash worried his bride had overdone it. Her color was *off,* and her smile no longer reached her eyes.

"Please, Cash, just let me enjoy—" Her face wrenched in pain, and he had to grab hold of her to even keep her upright.

"That's it…" Abandoning his cake plate on the table,

he guided his wife to the nearest willow chair. "Don't move an inch. I'm finding Doc Haven."

Wren hadn't wanted to believe she could be in early labor, but with each new contraction she feared that might be the case. Two weeks before her due date, her baby would be smaller than ideal, but still healthy.

"This better be good." All smiles, Doc Haven was clearly winded. "That's the most fun I've had dancing in at least thirty years. Delores does a mean two-step."

"I'm sorry Cash interrupted you. I'm sure these are—*ooh...*" Pain had her gripping the sides of her chair so hard that her nails dug into the soft wood.

"Wedding *and* a baby all in one day." Slapping Cash's back, the doctor said, "Good work, son." To Wren, he asked, "Can you make it to the nearest bedroom?"

"I—I think so...." She was all at once hot and cold. But on the inside. The pain was escalating. Almost more than she could bear.

"Wyatt!" Cash called to his brother. "Help me carry Wren to the guest room."

"Too much cake?" Wyatt asked. Unaware of the seriousness of the situation, he kept on with his shtick. "Maybe your stomach's too big from swallowing a watermelon? Or wait—brother Cash, did you have the honeymoon before the wedding and your bride's preggers?"

"Lay off," Cash ground out from between clenched teeth. "She's having our baby."

"Here? Now?" Wyatt paled. "I'm not so hot at this sort of thing."

"Would you shut up and grab the arm of her chair?" In case his daft brother still didn't grasp the plan, Cash pointed where Wyatt's hands should be.

A few minutes later Wren had been hefted onto the comfy canopy bed she'd napped on only hours earlier. "Doc Haven, why is this happening?"

"Who knows why anything happens when it does, dear." Easing extra pillows beneath her head, he said to Cash, "Fetch my bag from the back of my van. After that, have your mama boil water so I can sterilize my equipment. After that, come right back here. Your wife's going to need you. Oh—and I also need towels. Dozens, if you can find them."

"It hurts," Wren complained.

"I know," the doctor soothed. "Not sure how we're going to get you out of this dress, but let's try."

"I—I want Georgina. She'll know what to do."

When Cash returned with everything the doctor had requested, he was sent back out to put someone else on boiling-water duty.

"Honey," Georgina said, finally by her side, "Cash told me you asked for me? What can I do?"

"Please help me off with my dress. I want it pretty for m-my—" she rode out another contraction "—my own daughter."

"Good idea." As Wren had known Georgina would, she got straight to work unfastening rows of satin buttons on her back and sleeves.

Crying and laughing while shimmying out of the gargantuan gown, Wren managed, "Next time we're wedding-dress shopping, remind me to opt for cocktail length and Velcro."

"You got it," the older woman promised. "Only, let's hope that'll just be your vow renewal to my son."

A knock sounded on the door, and in walked Stella and Delores carrying a fancy, silver-wrapped box. "Pardon the interruption, Wren, but we thought this might be useful, if not exactly what it was originally intended for."

"C-could you please open it for me."

Inside was a peach chiffon nightgown and matching robe far too pretty to give birth in.

"I can't wear that," she complained.

"Of course you can." Delores assured her. "It's your wedding night, and even if you're not feeling your best, you should always look it."

"Ladies…" Doc Haven cleared his throat. "If you don't mind, it'd be helpful for me to get within at least a couple feet of my patient."

After much grumbling, Wren's two friends set off to make sandwiches for the guests, who'd all sobered enough to start a betting pool on the baby's sex and exact time of birth.

"All right." Tossing back the covers, the doctor said, "Now that we've got you dressed in something a little more appropriate, let's see how far along you really are."

Having already tucked towels beneath her and alongside her, Doc Haven performed his exam. "For a future doctor, you're not very in tune with your own body."

"Wh-what's that mean?" Indescribable pain rolled through Wren, making her want to pummel her gorgeous new husband for putting this baby inside her.

"Honey," Doc Haven noted, "you're fully dilated. It's time to push."

"B-but my water never broke."

"You should know as well as I do that sometimes that's the way it goes. Mother Nature doesn't want us knowing all the answers. This is going to be on your final exam, so listen up. What you're experiencing is a dry birth. Pretty rare, but I've seen it a few times. We'll get you through."

The pain had grown so intense Wren didn't know whether to scream or cry or both.

Georgina held her left hand and Cash her right. "Come on, honey, you can do it. Not much longer now. You were pretty lucky to have a wedding distract you from all of the long boring parts of giving birth."

"Arrgh." With all her might Wren pushed until she feared she'd black out.

"Good girl," Doc cheered. "A few more like that and we'll be in the baby business."

"D-did we remember to b-buy diapers?" Wren asked anyone who'd listen.

"Relax," Cash said. "Delores and some of her beauty-parlor friends bought us six months of cloth-diaper home delivery service."

"That was so *sweeeet.*"

"Uh-huh." Cash wiped her sweat-drenched forehead with a cold washcloth. "Breathe, sweetheart. Save your energy for pushing."

"I'm afraid we forgot a lot of stuff."

"Of course we did. That's why God invented grandmas. Right, Mom?"

"Absolutely."

"Less chitchat, more push." Doc Haven turned to Georgina. "She's crowning. Did anyone sterilize my surgical scissors?"

"They're on the towel on the dresser."

"Great." To Wren the doctor asked, "How about another push?"

"I don't think I can…." Thrashing her head, she fisted the sheets. "It hurts…it hurts."

"I love you," Cash said. "Hang in there, sweetheart. It'll be worth it. Just think of how good it's going to feel to hold our son in your arms."

"I hate you and we're having a *daughter!*" She used the vehemence behind what would hopefully be the end of this argument to be the fuel for her most powerful push.

"Almost there…"

Gritting her teeth, Wren fought to bring her baby into the world—and succeeded.

"Congratulations, newlyweds! You have a gorgeous baby girl."

"How's that possible?" Cash asked.

Georgina laughed, "Because God in all of His wisdom knows this family is desperate for females. I'm happy for you," she said to Wren. "She is lovely."

The doctor wrapped the baby in a blanket, resting her on Wren's chest. Transfixed, Wren couldn't stop staring. "Cash, look at her tiny fingers and toes."

"She's off-the-charts beautiful—like her mom…." He kissed Wren. "But I'm telling you now, no boy is ever getting near her."

"Slow down," the doctor said. "Let's tackle getting this charmer and her mama comfortable before you go pulling out the shotguns."

"THOUGHT YOU WANTED A BOY?" Wren crept up behind her husband, who stood at their daughter's crib, drinking her in. Two days had passed since her birth, yet Wren still couldn't believe she was really here.

"Hush it and revert back to our earlier conversation

on changing one's mind. She's perfect. Everything I ever wanted. She does, however, need a name." He stroked his daughter's perfectly pink cheek. "I was thinking Cashita. Cashalinda? Cashley?"

"Would you be serious," Wren scolded. "We've got to get her birth certificate and social security card." Wren's head spun just thinking about the amount of government paperwork.

Grinning over his shoulder, Cash reminded her, "Let's not forget to put her on waiting lists for all the best Weed Gulch preschools."

"You're awful." Taking his hand, she led him from the room. On the sofa, she resumed wrapping Christmas gifts—most of which had been ordered weeks earlier from the internet. "So? Names?"

He added another log to the fire. "Actually, you'll be happy to know I've put a lot of thought into this subject."

"Oh?" She cut a square piece of elf-themed paper.

"It makes me sad that our baby girl has no history on your side of the family. What she does have, however, is an awesome mom."

Eyes stinging, Wren said, "Thanks, but no need to butter me up. We're already married."

"Hear me out. My mom, and her mom, and even her mother's mom all share the same first initial and middle name—Marie. What if you did the same thing with our baby, only with bird names?"

"You're crazy." She put the singing-bass plaque Cash had selected for Dallas on the paper.

"A while ago—I think we were in the pool—you told me the women at your orphanage called you Wren because you were plain and sweet and never caused trouble. They made your middle name Katharine because one of them was a huge Katharine Hepburn fan and wanted you to eventually find that kind of brassiness for yourself. So what if we call our baby Robin Katharine Buckhorn. Thus combining pretty with sass and a last name that's become Oklahoma legend?"

"Robin…" Wren was beyond touched that Cash not only cared about their daughter's name having meaning, but that she knew from her first breath she was loved. "I like it. But what if the boys at school call her Robin the Robber? Or Batman and Robin?"

Cash punched his hand with his fist. "Dare one of them to try."

"It's official, then? We'll call her Robin Katharine Buckhorn?"

He held out his hand for her to shake, but then used her grip to pull her off the sofa and into his arms. "Didn't think you were getting off that easy, did you?"

"I hope not." When he pressed his lips to hers, no words described the champagne bubbles that seemed to have taken up permanent residence in her heart.

Without the baby between them, all mystery was gone when it came to how ready Cash was to finally pick up where they'd left off in Vegas. As soon as she got Doc Haven's okay, she planned to reacquaint herself with every one of Cash's gifts.

The more he kissed her, the more a sweet, aching hunger cried for more of him. Because he was now officially hers, she took the liberty of sliding her hands under his shirt and up his chest. His pecs were masterpieces in muscle, and before too long she removed the cloth barring her way from kissing every inch of him.

He groaned, easing his fingers into her hair. "You've got to stop."

"Why?" she teased, feigning innocence. "All I'm doing is this...." Kissing the line where his jeans hung low against his groin, she unfastened the top button, fully intent on giving her new husband a much-deserved *happy* ending.

AN HOUR'S WORTH OF FUN later, Wren woke to find herself having fallen asleep beside Cash on the sofa. "Hi."

"Yes, I am," he said with his grin. Playing with a strand of her hair, he asked, "When you first arrived at the ranch, did you ever dream we'd end up this happy?"

"No, but before you get too content with the status quo, we both have major hills to climb." Yawning, she managed to push herself onto her feet. Leaving him, she put a bow on Dallas's gift and set it under the twinkling tree.

"Like what? From where I'm sitting it all looks downhill from here. I'll get my knee fixed and go back out on the road. You get all those fancy initials added on to your name, then we pack up the munchkin—hell, we might have two or three more by then—and we'll all go on the road together. I'll buy us one of those tricked-out RVs. You'll love it. A lot of rodeo wives have them and swear they're like living in rolling mansions."

Freezing in front of the Christmas tree, Wren asked, "Did you think about a word you just said? Newsflash, but I never planned on spending ten years of my life to become a doctor, only to spend my life preggers and cheering from the sidelines while alternately praying I'm not watching the inevitable ride where you fall off a bull and never get up."

Chapter Sixteen

"I didn't mean it, okay?" Cash said later that night. Though he and Wren shared his king-size bed, as far as he was concerned he might as well have been sleeping with the ice chunk that'd taken over the front pasture pond. "Of course you'll do your doctor thing. When you can't, Mom can stay with Robin. Shoot, we could even pay Stella to take on our kiddo, too. Bottom line, we've got months and months till any of this comes to pass. Why are we fighting about it now?"

"Why?" Wren rolled to face him, in the process inadvertently knocking Prissy from her appointed pillow. The dog shot Cash a look nearly as offended as his wife's. "When we married, it was with the understanding that you not only knew how demanding my career is, but that you were fine with it. Now all of a sudden you're spinning cowboy fantasies of the *little woman* standing by her man."

"Ouch." Cash clutched his chest. "At least you'd be standing alongside a damned good-looking man—rich, too, once I get my sorry ass back on a bull."

Growling, she flopped back over. "You're impossible. Dense as that disgusting concoction you make for oatmeal whenever Mrs. Cahwood takes her days off."

Scooting over to her side of the bed, he spooned her, loving that her tummy now fit in his hand rather than the barn wheelbarrow. "Add bad cooking to my list of sins, but I'm still freakishly gorgeous, right?"

She hit him over the head with her pillow.

A WEEK AFTER ROBIN'S BIRTH, smack-dab in the center of the Woodland Hills Mall, Cash helplessly watched while the kid screamed bloody murder. He'd just bought her that year's special-edition Eskimo Joe's holiday T-shirt and tugged it over her little head. Hell, when he'd been a kid, he'd lived for this annual tradition. "What's wrong?"

"How should I know?" Wren jiggled the baby and rubbed her head, but nothing calmed her.

"You're supposed to be a doctor," Cash reminded her. "What good is your fancy degree if you don't know something as basic as why our baby's turning red?"

"Oh, dear..." A blue-haired onlooker shook her head.

Cash glared at the nosy old biddy.

Wren glared at him.

"What?" he asked, barely able to hear himself think.

"You should be nice to old people." Rocking and jiggling and cooing only infuriated Robin all the more.

"Seriously," Cash said to his new wife, growing more uncomfortable by the second as every passerby stared. "Do something."

"What would you suggest? I nursed her an hour ago. She already had her postlunch burp and poo. Want me to whip out a tranquilizer dart?"

Cash didn't appreciate Wren's sarcasm. "Aren't wives and new moms supposed to be pleasant?"

"If we weren't in the center of a crowded mall," she ground out from between clenched teeth, "I'd beat you silly."

"Nice, Wren." Hands on his forehead, Cash wished himself anywhere but his current location. "Our kid is dying and all you care about is smacking the crap out of me?"

"Robin's not dying," she growled, her pinched expression not as confident as her words.

With their wailing baby in the crook of one arm, she managed to steer the Mack truck of a stroller his mother had given them alongside a wooden bench. Unfortunately where Robin was concerned, adding sitting to her jiggling, rocking repertoire did little good.

"That crying is really getting to me," he confessed. "Mind if I go ahead and get back to shopping?"

"Y-you're kidding, right?" His clenched stomach told him Wren's narrowed eyes weren't a good thing.

Meanwhile, now even the kids in line for Santa pics had started to stare.

"Excuse me." A fellow mom with two sticky-faced toddlers rolled to a stop in front of Wren. "I see your baby has one of this year's Eskimo Joe's shirts. Did you check the inside of the tag? Last year my Lucy got one with a staple that poked her. Luckily she was old enough to tell me what was wrong."

Tugging the back of Robin's shirt, sure enough, Cash found the price tag had been stapled in place. It was positioned just right to stab his baby girl. In under ten seconds he had it removed and his daughter's screams faded to indignant "what took you so long" sniffles.

"Thank you," Wren said to the stranger. "I feel so

stupid. She's only a week old, and we're just starting to figure out her noises."

"Glad to help," the woman said, already on her way. "You'll get the hang of it."

Cash perched alongside Wren. "Looks like we flunked that parenting test."

"I feel awful." Nuzzling the side of Robin's head, Wren inspected the angry red scratch on her back. The staple hadn't broken the skin, but the way his baby girl had screamed, he'd have expected barbed wire sticking out of her tag.

Furious, Cash stood. "Wait here."

"Where are you going?" she asked while Robin sucked on her chubby fist.

"To give that store a piece of my mind. They can't just go around hurting children. Aren't there laws for this sort of thing?"

"Yeah." Smoothing her hand up and down the baby's back, Wren said, "There are also laws against bad parenting. We should've known to check the tag. In some of my prebaby reading, an article said the best way to prevent skin irritation is to remove tags."

Arms crossed, he asked, "Then why didn't you do it?"

"You seriously didn't just ask that." After easing their sleeping baby into her stroller, Wren was on her feet, weaving through the hellish holiday crowd.

Hands shoved in his jean pockets, Cash doggedly followed. "It's an honest question."

"Where?" she sassed over her shoulder. "In Cowboy Land? Surgical price-tag removal isn't taught. It's learned through firsthand parenting experience. Something neither of us have, but most especially you. Aside from changing a few diapers, what have you even done?"

"Plenty," he said as she entered a kitchenware store, maneuvering the stroller to a quiet side aisle. "I've changed diapers *and* made a late-night diaper run when we ran out of the cloth ones."

She put her hands on her hips, and mean flashed from her eyes. "Congratulations. I suppose that qualifies you for father of the year?"

"I'm trying, all right? And anyway, it's not like I can feed her. As for the whole bath thing..." He shook his head. "Nope. Not for me. She's tiny and slippery and if I accidentally hurt her, I don't know what I'd do."

Jaw hard, staring at the ceiling, Wren looked so far removed from the woman he felt he'd grown to know and married that had he been a sci-fi fan, he would've wondered if she'd undergone an alien switch.

"I'm sorry, okay?" His hands on her hips, finally able to ease in as close to her as he wanted, he brushed the pad of his thumb over her full lower lip. "I'm not sure what I'm apologizing for, but I obviously said bad, bad things. I deserve to be punished." She still wouldn't meet his gaze. "Seriously, spank me. Cuff me. Whatever you feel fits the crime." He winked and grinned, but it was tough working his charm without an audience. "If you'd look at me, my rugged sexiness would go a long way toward helping you select a proper punishment for my crimes."

Oh, she looked at him, all right, but not with lust— more like disgust.

Cash's stomach sank.

Had marrying Wren been the worst decision he'd ever made?

IT WAS CHRISTMAS EVE. The first ever Wren had experienced not with friends who took pity on her for being alone, but with a family truly her own—Robin. Her baby girl. Flawless in every way. Cash—her husband. The man she'd believed to be her best friend. If it hadn't been for the chill that'd settled between them ever since their disastrous shopping trip, she might have been happy. As it was, she felt trapped in limbo between a potential fairy tale and a nightmare.

In the kitchen late that afternoon, while Robin napped, Wren prepared a veggie tray to share that night with Cash's family.

Prissy lounged near her feet, eyes wide in hope of snagging a falling snack.

As she chopped cauliflower, Wren's memory regretfully wandered back to their mall outing. To their baby's crying. To the way once they'd discovered the problem, Cash had seemed furious with her for not having known what to do. His unrealistic expectations had been not only ridiculous, but cruel. As if because she'd been to medical school she should be a better parent than she currently was.

"Need help?" Fresh from the shower, Cash strolled into the kitchen with rumpled damp hair, wearing nothing but half-zipped jeans. Had she cared, she thought his six-pack abs would have qualified for the eighth world wonder. He stopped behind her, close enough for his radiant heat to muddle her thoughts. Wren pretended he'd never even entered the room.

"No, thank you."

He stole a baby carrot. "Wyatt's going to love this. When we were little, every holiday whenever we had a platter—cheese, meats, cookies, whatever—he used to sneak them from the table and run off to his room so he didn't have to share."

"Should I make two so he can have his own?"

Laughing, he said, "He does better with the whole sharing thing now than he used to."

She wanted to come up with some witty reply, but had nothing left in her to say. During their outing he'd really hurt her.

"We all right?" Cash nuzzled her neck, pressing warm, wet kisses in places he knew damned well turned her on. Maybe that was the problem with their whole stupid upside-down relationship. From the first night they'd met, he'd learned her every intimate secret. Now there was nowhere left for them to go.

"Honestly," she mumbled, resting her cheek against his chest, "I don't know. Your reaction at the mall was crushing. I wanted you to be jazzed that though we'd done it in an unorthodox way, together we figured out what was hurting our daughter and fixed it. Instead, I got the impression you blamed me from the start. That crack about me not learning about prickly tags in med school was not only uncalled for, it was insulting."

"I'm sorry." Judging by the darkening in his eyes, the lack of sexual innuendos, this time around he was sincere. "The munchkin's crying flipped me out. I wasn't prepared for that level of panic."

His raw confession touched her. She'd felt the same, but didn't think dads even cared about babies' crying. Oh, of course they cared, but not in the soul-deep way moms did.

"As for me not helping you out more on the late-night shifts, what do you want me to do?" He launched a heavenly shoulder massage. One that made her purr with contentment. Not that she wasn't still upset with him, but considering how much her back had been hurting, she put her fury on hiatus.

"All I want from you, Cash, is to know you're there. Half the time I'm sleepwalking, yet you don't seem fazed by Robin's attack on our schedule."

"Oh…" He pressed the heels of his hands to his eyes. "Trust me, I'm fazed, but again, I need guidance. When you're breastfeeding, I'm not even sure if I'm welcome in the room."

"Of course you are. Why wouldn't you be?"

"That's just it…" His back to her, he thumped the heel of his fist against the stainless steel fridge, and Prissy scampered to the living room. Cash continued, "When it was just me and you and occasionally my mom or Mrs. Cahwood around the house, I knew where I stood. I knew when you needed refills on herbal tea or when the flowers on your nightstand needed changing. Now, as much as I love Robin, I'm scared of her. She can't tell us what's wrong or what she needs." Taking over with the chopping of bite-size broccoli chunks, he added, "She reminds me of a Chinese exchange student Dallas brought home. We tried bending over backward to make the guy feel comfortable, but because of the language barrier, nothing worked. The week he was here felt like a start-to-finish disaster. Kind of like I feel as a father."

"First, comparing our daughter to a Chinese exchange student is crazy. Second, the more you're around Robin, the more instinct kicks in. By this time next week we'll both recognize the meaning behind her every burp and coo." Wren took mayo, buttermilk and sour cream from the fridge, intent on making homemade ranch dip for the center of her tray.

"How do you know?"

Artfully arranging black olives alongside celery, she noted, "Believe it or not, that's one area we did cover in med school."

Tackling the few dishes in the sink, he said, "I didn't mean to tick you off again."

"You didn't."

"Then why are you still refusing to look at me?"

Good question. One she suspected that were she to dwell on it for the next two weeks, she still wouldn't have an answer for. "Please," she implored, pushing stray hairs from her flushed cheeks, "can't we get through tonight and tomorrow without further deep discussion?"

Drying the cutting board he'd scrubbed, he turned to her, cracking a smile. "That mean you'd rather spend our time on more productive matters? Like making out?"

After the deep admissions they'd both shared, his reverting back to his usual carefree ways irked her to no end. Was the man ever serious? If not, was she willing to spend the rest of her life trying to tame him?

Chapter Seventeen

Christmas Eve, after their meal of turkey, ham and turducken with all the trimmings had been eaten, Cash sat with Wyatt and Dallas in his mom and brother's living room, watching a John Wayne movie marathon. Instead of a white Christmas, their part of the state had been slammed by pouring rain that showed no signs of letting up.

Robin, wearing a fuzzy green elf suit, had crashed on his chest. He loved how her eyelashes were already long enough to sweep her cheeks and every so often her little lips suckled.

"Been getting much sleep?" Dallas asked during a commercial for trash bags.

"Sure. Lucky for me, Wren's breastfeeding, so I usually get plenty of *zzzs*."

"Bad idea, man," Wyatt counseled. Prissy had long since crashed on his chest. "Friend of mine slept through every night feeding and found himself kicked to the curb after the kid's first birthday."

"Like you'd know," Cash argued. "You don't have a wife or kid."

"May well be…" Dallas sipped from his beer. "But this is one case in which I agree with Wyatt. You're playing a dangerous game in not sharing every part of the pleasure and pain of raising that baby girl."

"I change diapers."

Cash's oldest brother grunted. "Not nearly enough."

Tired of being nagged by the two guys he thought most likely to have his back, Cash picked up Robin and headed into the kitchen. Hopefully he'd fare better with leftovers and woman talk.

"Georgina," Cash overheard Wren saying, "he means the world to me, but how do I make him understand that so does earning my medical license and then joining— possibly even starting—my own practice?"

"Give it time. You two are just starting out. Adjusting to the baby and married life doesn't happen overnight."

Tiptoeing from the door he'd been hiding behind, Cash whispered to Robin, "Looks like Daddy needs to ramp up Mommy's Christmas surprise."

He took the back stairs two at a time. When he reached the twins' closed door, he slowly turned the knob and then crept the door open, inching his way inside.

"Who's there?" Bonnie asked, blinding him with the Barbie flashlight that had been in her stocking. Dallas being a softy where his girls were concerned, he'd allowed them to open one gift each and their stockings after dinner. "I've got an Old West sheriff rifle and I'll put on my badge and take you down!"

"Yeah," Betsy said, completing his twin torture by nailing him with her laser pointer. "I've got a hamster and I'll get him to go ninja on you!"

Robin started to cry.

"Ladies," Cash said, entering the room and closing

the door before turning on the lights, "who taught you to be so violent?"

"Uncle Cash!" Bounding out of their beds, the girls danced around him as if it'd been a year since their last visit.

"I wanna hold the baby," Bonnie demanded.

"No, me!" Betsy tugged Robin's foot.

Robin's scream was loud enough to wake the entire population of Weed Gulch.

"Knock it off," Cash said to the little monsters his brother was raising. "And keep your grubby paws off the baby."

"We're not grubby." Betsy was back to shining that damned laser thing in his eyes.

"Give me that." When he took it from her, she started to cry.

Bonnie kicked his shin.

Wincing in pain, but thankful she hadn't messed with his bum knee, he said, "You little bugger. Get back to bed pronto, or I'm calling Stella."

They feared their nanny far more than Dallas, who was the world's biggest pushover, so they scampered into their beds. After jiggling and patting Robin, Cash finally got her quiet, too.

"Now that everyone's settled down—" Cash perched on the foot of Betsy's bed "—I need a favor."

"I don't like you anymore," Bonnie announced.

"That's fine. Just give me your doctor kit."

"I *love* my doctor kit." Bonnie bolted back out of bed and sat on her toy box. "You can't have it."

"Please?" He wriggled Robin's arms to look as if she was begging, too. "I'll buy you a new one just as soon as I can get into town."

"What're you doing with it?" Betsy asked, plopping alongside her sister. "'Cause if you need to fix a broken gut or something, it doesn't *really* work."

Tired of sass, Cash placed Robin on Betsy's bed, surrounding her with pillows and animals so she wouldn't roll off. Next he hefted a twin under each arm and set them on Bonnie's bed. "Stay."

While the twins pouted, Cash rummaged through naked Barbies with chopped-off hair, missing limbs and eyeballs. Sparkle dresses and shoes and enough Lego to build a life-size house. Finally he found Bonnie's kit. It had been attacked with markers and crayons, but was basically still intact.

"Come on, munchkin." He scooped up Robin, glared at his nieces and said, "Wish Santa had known how ornery you two were before he bought your gift."

In unison, Betsy and Bonnie stuck out their tongues.

"Whew." After feeding Robin and tucking her into her crib, Wren collapsed on the sofa beside Cash. "Mothering is exhausting."

Prissy usually occupied the spot next to Wren, wherever that might be. But at the moment she was too busy with a chew bone to notice Cash horning in on her territory.

Lightly massaging Wren's neck, he asked, "Any thoughts on how you'll handle nursing once you're back at work?"

The question brought on an instant headache, as well as a hot rush of panic. Yes, she'd given the topic a lot of thought and with always the same result—how would she realistically have it all? Marriage? Motherhood? The career as a doctor she'd worked years to achieve? It felt just within her reach, if only she were smart enough, energetic enough, stubborn enough to juggle it all.

"Well..." She forced her breathing to slow. "Since the day care is on-site, I'll pop in to feed Robin whenever possible. If that doesn't work, I can always pump milk or supplement with formula."

"And us?" He shifted on the sofa, his proximity making it impossible for her to look anywhere but at him. At those gorgeous green eyes that had first drawn her in. Since having Robin, Wren had harbored horrible thoughts of wondering where she'd be now if she'd never met him. Midway through her first year of residency would she be happier? More fulfilled? Or was it the exhaustion of new motherhood forcing her thoughts to gloomy places?

"Cash..." How did she begin sharing her thoughts with him? No man wanted to hear his wife of barely two weeks already confessing doubts about their future. "I'm tired. We have Christmas with your family in the morning. Do we have to have this conversation now?"

"No. Sorry." He smiled, but even having known him as briefly as she had, Wren knew by his lack of dimples that his heart wasn't behind the expression.

"Ready for bed?"

"Actually—" he nodded toward the Christmas tree "—while you were with the baby, Santa left you an early gift." He presented the simply wrapped box with a flourish. "He advised me to give it to you now, before the family crush. Besides, after the past few rocky days, I wanted to..." Voice cracking, he looked away. "Look, I've been an ass. Said things I regret, and I'm sorry. Considering where we are in our relationship, this gift is backward, but…" He nodded toward the box. "Go ahead. Open it."

In the months Wren had lived with Cash, she couldn't remember him being more humble. Cupping her hand to his dear cheek, more than anything she wished she could've met him five years down the road. By then she would've been established. Ready for more than the one hot night they'd intended to be all they'd ever share. Now, even though she wasn't sure, she felt caged by circumstance. She needed to file for her residency transfer, but couldn't get Dr. West's voice from her head. *I've lost a lot of promising candidates due to so-called love, and I refuse to lose you, Wren Barnes.*

Not that Wren hadn't known full well what she'd been doing when she married Cash, but she felt as though she now had the stomachache of a child who'd eaten too much candy when her entire life before meeting him had been sugar free. Was what she shared with Cash the real deal or her mentor's *so-called* love?

And then Cash melted her heart as if it had been made of chocolate. Inside the box was an obviously well loved child's doctor kit just like the one she'd had at the orphanage. Only, the stethoscope on this model included a spellbinding square-cut diamond ring.

On his knees in front of her, Cash said, "You should've had this before our wedding, but I hope you'll forgive me enough to not only wear my engagement ring, but honor me by becoming the first full-fledged doctor in the Buckhorn clan." After slipping it onto her trembling left ring finger, he kissed it. He then rose to kiss her lips.

"Th-thank you," she said, voice husky, eyes shining. "It's beautiful, but Cash, it's also unnecessary. I don't need a ring to seal me to you."

Rising, he threw his hands in the air. "Dammit, I'm not trying to *buy* you, but show you I care. I'm going to be a better father to Robin. A better husband to you. I'm sick of bickering and—"

Wren crushed him in a hug. "I've been so afraid that since we're married, you expect me to give up my career to raise Robin on my own. Don't get me wrong, I love everything about being a mother, but…"

"I get it," he explained, raining kisses over her cheeks and brows and finally, deliciously, her lips. "I'm going ahead with my surgery. You're going ahead with your residency. Together, we'll be unstoppable."

She wanted to believe him. Oh, how she wanted to trust in Cash's every word, but more than anyone, Wren knew dreams rarely—if ever—came true.

"THANK YOU, UNCLE CASH and Aunt Wren!" Upon unwrapping their kid-sized, battery-powered Hummer, Dallas's twins wriggled and screamed to such a degree Cash was afraid they'd wake Robin, who was finally asleep in the portable crib his mother had set up in a relatively quiet corner of the main house's living room.

Prissy wriggled along with them, but then found a candy cane and snuck off with it under the couch.

"You're welcome," Cash said, hugging them both, "but please, keep the celebrating quiet."

"Okay!" The girls' exaggerated whisper was hardly an improvement.

"Can we drive it now?" Bonnie asked.

"Let's go to the mall," Betsy said.

"And get ice cream." Bonnie ripped at the supersized box.

"Slow down," their father said. "The end of the driveway is as far as you two will be traveling."

With both girls pouting, Georgina said, "Wren, I wasn't sure about your size, so if your blouse doesn't fit, I have the receipt. It's from the cutest Utica Square boutique. If you need to take it back, we'll do lunch."

"Sounds fun," Wren said, fingering the white silk blouse Cash's mom had given her, "but it's so beautiful, I'm hoping it looks great."

"Ladies never need an excuse to do lunch," Georgina noted, gathering the crumpled wrapping at her feet.

Wren laughed, helping with the cleanup. "Thank you, everyone, for such a fun morning. I've never had a family Christmas, and..." Seeing his wife choked up formed a knot in Cash's throat. Waving her hands in front of her suddenly red face, she managed to say, "You all are amazing. I'm lucky to have found you."

"Feeling's mutual," Georgina said, practically pushing Cash to give his wife a hug. "I'm so glad you've decided to stay with us. I realize even with your residency in Tulsa you'll still be busy, but at least we'll see you every once in a while."

Cash witnessed Wren's smile fade to a frown. What was she thinking? Was she sad about her change in plans? Would she grow to resent him for it? Or worse yet, did she already? On the surface, everything between them had never been better. They shared meals and jokes and he'd been doing more diaper changes on Robin. What more did Wren want from him?

Dallas patted Cash's shoulder. "Love the new fly-fishing gear."

"Good." Cash wanted to say more, but at the moment didn't have it in him.

"Wanna give me a hand?" Wyatt nodded toward both of them to help get the Hummer from the box.

With the twins dancing around their gift, his mother and Wren cleaning and Stella with her own family in Stillwater, the old place felt almost as it had back when his father had still been alive. What would Duke say about Cash's predicament? Would he think his son was overreacting? Was now the time for Cash to man up and tell Wren how things between them were going to be? Her transferring her residency would be best for not only him, but Robin. Surely she knew that, so why was she apparently still riding the proverbial fence?

"IT'S DONE." HAVING set his knee surgery appointment for a few days after New Year's, Cash hung up the phone.

"How do you feel?" Wren asked from the living-room sofa, where she nursed Robin.

Prissy protectively sat beside them.

"With all this rain, my knee hurts like hell."

Making a face, she said, "That's not what I meant. Are you satisfied you've made the right decision?"

"What other decision is there? Either I have surgery or I'm off the tour."

She switched Robin to her other breast. "I'm hardly an orthopedic surgeon, but once you heal, you should be good as new."

Grunting, he stared out the window at the puddles forming on the drive. "Never thought I'd say this, but lately I've been wondering if that's what I want. You know, to be good as new? Before I had a family of my own, I used to feel invincible. Now I worry if something happens to me, where does that leave you and our baby girl?"

"Good question. Not gonna lie, but I worry about you getting hurt again—only next time, worse." Robin had fallen asleep at her breast. Wren repositioned the baby, tugging up the flap of her nursing bra and pulling down her T-shirt. "I'm a big girl. I'd survive without you."

"Gee, thanks." He looked away from her in disgust.

Securing Robin on the sofa with a wall of pillows, Prissy on the opposite end lightly snoring, Wren slipped her arms around him, resting her cheek on his chest. "That's not what I meant and you know it. What I was trying unsuccessfully to convey is that I know how much riding means to you. I would never ask you to give it up in order to give me a false sense of security. Let's pretend you quit riding and worked the ranch full-time. Who's to say you couldn't be just as badly injured falling off a horse or being maimed in some—" she tossed up her hands "—I don't know, some rattlesnake attack?"

"Did I truly marry that much of a city girl?" He kissed the bridge of her nose.

"It could happen. Snakes attack, don't they?"

"Sure, but typically not unprovoked. Certainly not en masse."

"Yet it *could* happen?" She played with the ribbing around the collar of his T-shirt, unwittingly turning him on with the soft backs of her nimble fingers. Cash could've strangled the physician who had invented the "no sex for at least six weeks after having babies" rule.

"Honey," he said with a low growl, "for you, I would do my damnedest to move the stars, but I would hope you wouldn't want me to coordinate a snake attack for the sole reason of proving you right."

"No, thank you." Smiling sweetly up at him, she said, "Although I suppose if you get tired of riding bulls, you could always try your hand at a carnival sideshow featuring various fanged creatures."

"The only freaky sideshow I want to star in," he said along with his most charming grin, "would feature you and our bed—without your attached-at-the-hip dog."

"Three, two, one...Happy New Year!"

On her tiptoes, Wren kissed her husband, tuning out the crowd around them. Georgina loved a party, and in true Buckhorn style, half the town had shown up to ring in the New Year.

Streamers and champagne flowed. Balloons and confetti and noisemakers accompanied the same country band that had played at Wren and Cash's wedding. "Auld Lang Syne" performed with fiddles took on a slow, reminiscent quality that quieted the once-boisterous crowd.

"A year ago," Cash said, hands on her hips, swaying her in time to the music, "would you have ever believed we'd be married with a dog and a baby?"

"Would've been tough, considering I didn't even know you a year ago."

"So true." He returned her kiss. "Guess that's why you're the brains of this organization."

"Don't you forget it." Standing in his arms, Wren

would have been hard-pressed to remember her life before meeting him. He made her feel safe and adored. Yes, they'd had their issues, but lately, the more he helped with Robin and the more affectionate they'd become, the more she found herself wanting to be with him night and day.

"What's your resolution?" he asked.

Up until now she hadn't given it much thought. "I suppose I should be more productive. Since moving in with you, I've turned into quite the slug."

"At least you're an attractive one." As Cash gripped her tighter, Wren reveled in his all-male form against her. Unlike her, the man didn't have an ounce of fat on him. His every inch had been honed to perfection, partially in his home gym, but mostly from plenty of hard outdoors work.

"Mmm…" She snuggled closer. "Right back atcha." After a few moments more dancing, she asked, "How about you? Any special goals for the coming year?"

"I want to be a really great dad. My own father had some amazing qualities, but I always felt pretty far down on his to-do list. Robin needs to know that she and her mother come first."

Cash's words warmed Wren through and through.

They also worried her. Though she and the great Duke Buckhorn had never met, she suspected they shared the same level of determination. Now that she'd held Robin in her arms and assumed her daily care, Wren realized just how difficult raising her child and completing her residency would be. She knew quite a few guys in her program who had kids, but they also had wives to care for them. Come to think of it, she couldn't name a single other woman in her particular residency program with kids. Not even Dr. Abigail West, the world-renowned heart surgeon. Her lack of family was the price she'd chosen to pay for success. But was Wren willing to go that far? She hadn't even summoned the courage to complete her transfer forms.

"Tired?" Cash asked when Wren turned quiet.

She nodded.

Robin had long ago conked out in the twins' room in her portable crib.

"It's been a wonderful night," Wren said. "Special in every way." Aside from nagging worries about her residency that refused to release her.

"Not *every* way," he whispered in her ear, his warm voice making her shiver. The thought of being with him again brought on a hot and dizzy rush. His raw sex appeal had been what had landed her in this mess in the first place. But then, looking back at the past nine months, was Robin a mess? Of course not.

And your marriage?

Caressing the base of her throat, Cash kissed her deeply enough for Wren to feel it in her toes. Her whole body hummed with awareness. His merest touch made her feel electrified. As if every inch of her body had been massaged to a hypersensitive glow.

Was this love? Having never before experienced it, how did she know?

Chapter Eighteen

"Sure you have enough food?" January 3 in the black before dawn, Georgina stood alongside Cash's truck wringing her hands as if he were going off to war.

"Mom," he said, "I'm having a simple outpatient surgery done by one of the best knee guys in the whole damned country. Hell, if his work fails, I've got my own doc right here." Reaching behind the already snoozing munchkin in her car seat, Cash gave Wren's shoulder a squeeze.

"I know," his mother said, "but I still feel like I should be with you."

"You're welcome to ride along, but with all of Robin's gear, you'd have to sit in the back." Grinning, he nodded toward the truck's bed.

Judging by her crossed arms and pressed lips, his mother didn't find him amusing. "You know I've always hated your bull riding. Your cocky nothing-can-hurt-me attitude is just one more reason why."

"On that note..." Cash started the engine.

"Wren," his mother called past him, "you call with regular updates."

"I will," his wife promised.

Five hours later they'd reached the office of the orthopedic surgeon his team doctor had recommended.

Next came an hour's worth of paperwork and changing into a blue-striped dress that would show off his ass to any and all who cared to look.

His surgeon stopped in for a visit, explaining in a little too much detail exactly what he planned to do. By this time, Cash wanted the damned thing over and done with. It was long since time to get back to work.

Through all of this, Wren struck him as strangely silent. Not so much nervous, but melancholy. As if she'd lost her favorite pirate book. Was worry about him what had put the furrow between her eyebrows?

"Baby, I'm going to be fine," he assured her, taking her hand in his.

"I know." She jiggled Robin, who was wide-eyed and drooling at the bright lights of her new surroundings.

"Then why can't you smile for me?"

She forced it, but even a dumbo bull rider like himself knew she was faking. "Sweetie, seriously, before you know it, I'll be sprung from here, taking you out to a fancy early supper."

"Uh-huh." Rising, she managed to hold Robin with one arm while still fussing with his blankets. "I appreciate the thought, but I'm taking you straight home. You're going to hate me once we start your range-of-motion exercises."

"I could never hate you." Gazing upon his wife and child did funny things to his chest. He felt a squeezing pressure, but not in a bad way. More as if he didn't know where he left off and they began. As if without them, he might survive, but never again thrive. "Come here."

Wren perched on the edge of his gurney-style bed. "You should rest."

Slipping his hand beneath her hair, he pulled her in for a kiss. "You should stop being bossy long enough for me to tell you I love you." It was the first time he'd told her since she'd been in labor. That time, she'd declared hatred for him, which, considering her pain, he hadn't blamed her for, but this time he wanted more.

"I—I think I love you, too." Laughing, maybe even crying a little, she added, "Sorry, that came out wrong. Honestly, you're the first man I've ever said those words to."

"Kiss me," he demanded. Fortunately for him, she for once did as she was told and did a properly hot job of sending him off for medicinal torture.

"Whoa…" Cash's nurse bounded into his curtained cubicle, only to shield her eyes with his chart. "Should I come back later?"

"We're good," he assured her, wishing he'd had a few more minutes alone with Wren, but eager to get on with the next phase of his life.

"Great," the tall blonde said with enough exuberance to make him wonder if she'd been a college cheerleader. "Let's go fix your knee."

PACING WHILE ROBIN NAPPED in her carrier, Wren could scarcely contain her emotions. Back and forth she traveled across fawn-colored carpet so thick her footfalls made no sound. Upholstered red leather chairs held two other people. Calmly reading magazines, they didn't look half as nervous as she felt.

Before she'd seen Cash wheeled away, surgical procedures had seemed to her like high-tech video games.

Patients hadn't been real, but more like characters presenting problems for her to study.

The practical side of her knew Cash would be in recovery in just over ninety minutes. She knew after that he'd face painful rehabilitation, but a probable full recovery. He'd return to his bull riding and she…

What would she do?

Did Tulsa hold the same opportunities as Baltimore? What about Weed Gulch? After all, staying with Cash meant living with him on the ranch. He'd never leave it, and she'd never have the gall to ask him.

Warding off a sudden chill, Wren hugged herself. Cash's unexpected declaration of love hadn't lightened her heavy heart. Having had a family as well as countless lovers, Cash had the advantage of at least knowing the word's definition.

Despite that fact, it took only a glance at her sleeping child to remind Wren that she was on the fast track to achieving her every familial dream.

Minutes ticked into an hour and then more. Finally Cash's surgeon sauntered into the waiting area. When he smiled, relief shimmered through her.

"Cowboy Cash did great. I want him in recovery at least a couple of hours, and then you can take him home."

"Thank you," she said, almost afraid to stand for fear of her shaky knees giving out. "Any special aftercare?"

"My nurse will give you an instruction packet. I want his brace on with an ice pack for the first five days. He'll need to be up on crutches ASAP, contracting his thigh muscles, rotating his feet—it's all in the packet." The surgeon held out his hand for her to shake. "Also, I'll give you the number of my favorite physical therapist up in your neck of the woods."

Mouth dry, mind overwhelmed, Wren nodded.

What was wrong with her?

"Have a safe trip home." Just as abruptly as he'd arrived, the man was gone. Wren had worked herself into such an emotional state, she couldn't even remember the surgeon's name.

Before having Robin, before meeting Cash, orthopedics had been one of the residency rotations she'd most looked forward to. Now she just wanted to see her husband.

The notion was all at once thrilling and terrifying.

Her entire life she'd leaned on no one but herself, and had been successful. She'd lived by the principle that being on her own was streamlined efficiency at its best.

Upon returning to her residency, she'd have neither time nor energy for Robin, let alone Cash. The presumption wasn't some pie-in-the-sky ideal, but fact. How did she meld the two halves of her new life? Was it even possible?

After she called Georgina and Mrs. Cahwood to share the news that Cash's surgery had gone well, adrenaline turned to exhaustion, forcing Wren back into her chair. Movie magazine in hand, she thumbed through starlets' dresses and managed to read a piece on the latest Hollywood scandal before her eyes drifted shut.

"Mrs. Buckhorn?" Two hours later a nurse jolted Wren from a light sleep. "Your husband's awake and asking for you."

It took Wren a minute to gather Robin's things and her purse. After that, she followed the nurse down a short maze of brightly lit halls, finally entering the quiet area reserved for patients returning to consciousness from general anesthesia.

"Hey, gorgeous," Cash said with just enough potency behind his handsome grin to make her eyes sting with relief. "Hope you brought mashed potatoes."

"Sorry," she said, holding Robin close while leaning over to kiss his forehead, "my purse happens to be fresh out, but I'll call Mrs. Cahwood to put in your request."

With a sleepy, smiley nod, he drifted back to sleep.

"Wake up," she coaxed with a gentle nudge. "I want you out of here."

"Did our bags make it all right?"

"What?" Wren laughed at Cash's latest drug-induced question.

"Can't start our Vegas honeymoon without my wife having her suitcase." Eyes already closed, he added, "It's a secret, so don't tell her you know."

TWO DAYS LATER CASH WOKE to his knee still feeling as if he'd wrestled with a hundred hornets and lost.

"Wren!" he hollered from their room.

She bustled in with Robin.

Prissy followed, looking none too happy about the baby taking her usual spot in Wren's arms.

Wren said, "Breakfast is almost done."

He winced. "I need something for pain."

"I want you to take it with something to eat, so you'll need to wait about five minutes."

Trying to shift positions and only causing more burning agony, he growled.

"How did you cope with pain while riding?"

"That was different. A man can't show he's a wuss in front of thousands of people."

"Uh-huh…" Wren plopped the baby next to him on the comforter before making a nuisance of herself by fluffing his pillows.

Robin fussed.

Cash tried reaching to comfort her, but couldn't quite pull it off.

"Let me," Wren said, snatching her up. "You rest."

"I'm tired of resting."

"Want me to turn on the TV?" Wyatt had needed a part for one of the oil rigs, which had called for a trip to Tulsa. Since he'd been only a few miles from an electronics store, Cash had coerced him into picking up the new flat screen now parked atop the dresser.

"No, thanks."

"Other than a pain pill and breakfast, what do you want?"

He sighed. "To feel normal again. Do you have any idea how long it's been since I've put in a full day's training? Or even helped Dallas with the ranch?" Judging by her hasty look away from him and out the wall of bedroom windows, she knew exactly how long it'd been since either of them had worked at anything besides caring for her, then newborn Robin and now him. Were their lives forever destined to stagnate in this holding pattern?

"I'm as frustrated as you, but it won't be too long until you're on a busy rehabilitation schedule." Her back to him, with Robin calmed and resettled on the bed, she began putting up the clean clothes overflowing the laundry basket. "Plus, I'm not exactly thrilled with this situation, either."

"Way to make a man feel loved." Was he imagining things, or for a fraction of a second after his quip, did she freeze? As if she hadn't viewed his joke as all that amusing. *Did* she love him? She'd sure shown him in a hundred ways. By nursing him around the clock. Doting on their daughter and dog. Those kinds of things were enough to prove love, right? He was hardly insecure enough to need something as lame as a verbal confirmation.

"I've been thinking…" Continuing with her task, she said, "Though you may not believe it now, by the end of the week you'll be off your crutches and busy with strengthening exercises."

Why did his stomach now hurt more than his knee? "What are you saying?"

"We'd planned for me to resume my residency in February."

"Yeah, but in Tulsa, right?"

Either she hadn't heard him or was deliberately ignoring him. Knowing her as he did, he voted for the latter.

"What's going through that pretty head of yours?"

She tucked her bras into his sock drawer—his tip-off that something was going on.

"Talk to me, Wren."

"I'm fed up, okay?" She spun to face him. "Your whole life you've been programmed to care for dozens of people. Your mom and dad. Brothers and sister. Neighbors and friends. I'm a loner, and all of this domestic bliss is getting on my nerves."

Liar. In his esteemed opinion, she was scared. But that was okay. He had enough love in him to see all three of them through. He might've been out of it after his surgery, but he also remembered her shining eyes. The way she'd sweetly kissed him—as if he'd been a dream she was afraid would fade away.

Trying to lighten the mood, he asked, "I don't suppose I could trouble you for breakfast and a pain pill before you go?"

"I'm sorry." Face reddening, she crushed him in a hug. "I don't know what got into me."

"It's all right," he assured her. "Between your pregnancy and my knee, we've both been at this bed-rest thing for too long."

"Speaking of which..." Reclining on her side of the king-size mattress, Wren tickled Robin's chubby tummy. "Not sure if you remember or not, but when you were waking from surgery, you spilled the beans on a Vegas trip. Was that for real or drug-induced rambling?"

Stomach hurting again, only for a much different reason, he asked, "Am I going to be in trouble if I confess to ignorance?"

She shook her head.

"I'd like to take you. Have to admit it sounds fun. We could book the same room." He winked. "Reenact our first night together."

"On that note—" she sat up "—I'm off to get your breakfast. Need me to take the baby?"

"Leave her. She's a good distraction."

His wife flashed a pinched smile before closing the bedroom door. Hard to believe a few minutes earlier, his throbbing knee had been his only problem. Now he was also left to dwell on not only what Wren wasn't telling him, but how he was going to find out.

In Cash's study with the door closed, well away from the prying eyes and ears of not only her husband, but Mrs. Cahwood, Wren's hand's trembled to such a degree she had difficulty punching Abigail's private cell number into the phone.

Wren had hoped her talk with Cash would've gone better, but then, how could it when she feared he wasn't going to like what she had to say?

"Happy baby, Miss Barnes!" her friend uncharacteristically gushed after two rings, no doubt recognizing the Oklahoma number on her caller ID. "When am I going to see you? Sometimes I feel like you were the only competent candidate on our team."

"Actually, that's why I called." Though flattered, Wren knew Abigail's complaint was pure fiction, considering the *team* consisted of ten of the brightest young medical minds in the country. "I spoke with the dean about a possible transfer to University of Oklahoma's Tulsa residency program. He sent the papers a while back, but I have yet to sign them."

"I thought that was a joke." In her mind's eye Wren saw the always perfectly dressed, unflappable surgeon seated behind her French provincial desk, no doubt multitasking as she talked. "I'm sure Oklahoma produces fine physicians, but Wren, you and I both know you're special. Destined for greatness that can only be fostered by greatness. That sort of training can only be found in a handful of programs. Ours happens to be one of them. There's a reason you haven't filled out those transfer forms. Deep down, you know I'm right."

Twirling a pencil between her fingers, Wren searched for a legitimate argument, but came up lacking.

"Now, the committee agrees that due to your pregnancy, you've missed too much of your first year to make up. No worries, though, as I've already found you a plum research position. Really top-notch, which you'll be able to start right away. Meaning, you've been hiding out on the prairie long enough. I want you and baby back here pronto. You're even welcome to stay with me, which I wish I'd suggested in the first place before you took off for the wilds. I should've hired a private medical jet to safely carry you home." Barely pausing for breath, she added, "What's done is done. All that matters now is making up for lost time. Tell me your address and I'll send you and baby your itinerary and flight information. Do babies fly free?" Laughing, she said, "I have no idea, but my secretary should know."

"Dr. West—Abigail…" Wren's mouth was so dry, her tongue could barely move. Her mentor held the key to her every dream. Even her housing problem had been magically whisked away. Abigail had taken on the role of her fairy godmother and as such, seemed determined to knock down any obstacle. Little did she know Wren's only roadblock happened to be a husband.

"Sorry to cut this short. I didn't realize the time, and I'm due in surgery in ten. Let me transfer you to Eloise and she'll get your address."

After a brief conversation with the secretary that basically consisted of turning traitor on her new family, Wren hung up the phone.

Chapter Nineteen

On crutches, six days after his surgery, Cash hobbled from the front door to the barn, trying not to squash Prissy in the process. The mutt danced around him, growling at the metal frames as if they were dragons. His knee still throbbed, but it felt great to be out of bed and into bright sun. Though the temperature was barely fifty, his efforts already had him working up a sweat.

"You're doing great, sweetheart." Wren, with a bundled-up Robin in her arms, walked alongside him. "Don't be afraid to admit you need to rest."

"No way," he said through gritted teeth. "I'm going for it." His body said otherwise. Refusing to give in to the pain, he split the difference by leaning back on his crutches.

Out on the dirt road a dust cloud rose, caused by a speeding FedEx truck.

"There's something you don't see every day," he noted. When the vehicle turned onto their drive, he asked, "You order something?"

Her face paled. "No."

"Maybe he's headed for the main house and took a wrong turn?"

The driver parked and hopped out. "Morning. Either of you Wren Barnes?"

"She's Wren Buckhorn." Grinning, still resting on his crutches, Cash hooked his thumb in his wife's direction. "Guess someone didn't get the memo about our wedding."

Not looking amused, the driver held out a computerized clipboard for Wren to sign.

She did.

The driver in turn handed over a ten-by-thirteen envelope. "Have a great day."

"Who's it from?" Cash asked, peeking over her shoulder. Unfortunately, Robin blocked his view.

"It's no doubt paperwork on my residency transfer."

"Open it," he urged, more than ready for her stay in Oklahoma to become officially permanent.

"Later. Now you have work to do." Smacking his butt with her package, she said, "Come on, get moving to the barn."

Midway there, Robin began to fuss.

"What's wrong?" Cash asked their daughter in a coochie-coo tone.

Wrinkling her nose, Wren said, "Surprise! Your baby left a smelly package for you."

"Not me." Hustling toward his goal, he said, "Remember? I've got more work to do."

"Will you be okay on your own?" Her furrowed brow didn't show much faith in his hobbling skills.

"I'm fine," he promised. "Go ahead and get her changed. I smell her from here."

IN THE HOUSE, Wren quickly changed Robin's diaper before placing her in her living-room playpen. After a hand wash, Wren sat on the sofa with her envelope. Abigail's return address already had her dreading the contents.

She'd just torn the zip closure when Cash fumbled through the door, Prissy leading the way.

"How's that for record timing?" he asked with the same broad smile that had first drawn her to him so many months ago.

"I'm impressed." She was also finding it hard to breathe now that his growing efficiency with his crutches had him already across the room, collapsing onto the sofa beside her. "Good job."

"Thanks." He seemed expectant. As if he wanted something.

"Thirsty?" she asked, already rising. "Need me to take off your shoes?"

"What's in the envelope, Wren?"

If her heart raced any faster, she'd keel over. "I—I already told you I don't know."

Sighing, he raked his fingers through his hair. "In all the time we've been together, I don't think you've ever just out-and-out lied to me. Why start now?"

She wanted to continue the lie indefinitely, but couldn't. It wasn't fair to him or his family, who had been nothing but welcoming to her from practically her first day on the ranch. Yes, she and Georgina had gotten off to a rocky start, but now that Wren was a mother, she understood why her mother-in-law had been so preoccupied with the interests of Cash and her future grandchild.

"Talk to me." He took her hand, tracing the outline of her fingers. "What could be so bad?"

"I—I have to go." Tears streamed down her cheeks,

hot and messy and strangely quiet. As if the pain stemmed from so deep inside her that the secret place had never before been exposed.

"Go where, honey?"

"Back to Baltimore. I never even applied for a transfer. I started to—many times—but couldn't. The chance to one day work with Dr. West is just too rare."

"And you and me and Robin? What we have isn't rare?"

"Cash, please…" Still crying, she struggled with a way to make him understand just how much she hated doing this to not only him, but herself. "My leaving is for the best. I've been fooling myself in ever thinking the two of us could last anywhere near forever. Since the day we first met, I've told you I'm a loner. I just wasn't made for a shared life."

He didn't look at her. Didn't move a muscle other than an errant nerve ticking in his jaw.

"When you were in surgery," she said, "it destroyed me. And that was a relatively minor thing. I would die should something more serious ever happen—like I permanently lose you."

After a sharp laugh, he said, "So instead of letting fate take its course, like most sane married couples do, you're grabbing the bull by the horns and just leaving me?"

"It's not that simple," she tried to explain. "My whole career is at stake. Everything I've worked so hard for."

This time when he pushed himself up, he stayed on his feet while reaching for his crutches.

"You should rest," Wren advised. "After such a long walk, you have to be exhausted."

"Don't," he ground out. "Don't you dare pretend to care."

"I do. You mean the world to me. I—" *I love you.* Trouble was, she wasn't even sure what the words meant. Life experience had taught her love equals pain. Growing attached to someone or something equaled eventual loss. It was as simple as that. Why couldn't Cash understand?

"How long have you been planning this escape?"

Raising her chin, she admitted, "From the day I set foot on your property."

"Why'd you even bother marrying me? Other than making me out to be a fool?"

"I don't know." Covering her face with her hands, she now knew that to be true. At the time she'd been caught up in the romance of it all. The cake and gorgeous white dress. The fairy-tale hope that maybe just this once, dreams really would come true. But then she'd talked to Abigail and realized her actual dreams resided back in Baltimore. With the goals she'd held dear ever since playing doctor on her little dog Waldo all those years ago.

"I suppose you're taking the baby?" he asked.

"Of course. I'm still breastfeeding."

"All right, then." Hobbling toward the back door, he said, "Let me know when you need a ride to the airport. I'll make sure there's someone around to drive you."

His cold demeanor was more than she could bear.

"Please, Cash…" She went to him, put her arms around him, expecting his usual strong embrace. The one that made her feel safe and secure and capable of meeting any goal she'd ever dreamed of achieving. But instead of wrapping his arms around her, he stood ramrod still, hands curved tight around his crutch handles. "Talk to me," she begged. "Tell me you still want to spend time with Robin and me during your touring breaks."

"Right now," he cruelly noted, "I'd gladly see my daughter every day. As for you, I'd probably get along just fine never setting eyes on you again."

AT FIVE THE NEXT MORNING, the lights from Henry's pickup shone through the front windows.

Having been up most of the night tossing and turning in the guest bed, Wren stood in the living room waiting. Robin slept in the carrier portion of her car seat that Cash had informed her he'd already switched to the foreman's truck. Prissy also slept, only in her designer pooch purse.

Her actions braver than her emotions, Wren mechanically walked toward the door, telling herself she'd made the right decision for her daughter and her. The opportunities for Robin in Baltimore would be limitless. Here in Weed Gulch she'd be lucky to win a spelling bee, let alone a prestigious debate title or science scholarship.

"Sure you want to do this?" Henry asked when Wren opened the door.

Not sure at all, she went through the motions, assuring him in a falsely bright tone that if she wanted to be a doctor, returning to Baltimore was her only option.

Wren had hoped Cash would at least step out of the room they used to share long enough to say goodbye, but he didn't.

And so she left, leaving behind no traces she'd ever been there save for Robin's crib and changing table and the light floral scent of her own perfume in the air.

The ride to the airport was uneventful.

Henry wasn't the talkative sort, and Wren was thankful for the fact. Pulling up to the curb nearest her airline, he unloaded everything, slipped the porter a twenty and then with the slightest tip of his hat, climbed back behind the wheel and drove off.

Standing in the surprisingly long security line, Wren reflected on how many people she'd hurt by not at least saying goodbye. Georgina and Stella. Delores, Mrs. Cahwood and Doc Haven. Even Dallas and Wyatt and the twins. Surely she'd see all of them again. After all, they were family.

Then why are you leaving?

The question hit from nowhere with the force of an Oklahoma twister to her gut. Had it not been for the knowledge that Abigail was expecting her in Baltimore, Wren might've called Cash, begging him to forgive her for putting a stupid job before their marriage. But then she came to her senses. Becoming a doctor was a goal she'd worked hard for. It wasn't stupid, but noble. Once licensed, she knew she'd be able to do good for so many people, rather than merely a few.

Having convinced herself that her deep affection for Cash, his family and their friends had been a fleeting thing, she edged forward in the suddenly moving line. And when she thought she saw her husband out of the corner of her eye near a coffee stand, she chalked it up to exhaustion. Instead of admitting that in reality, her seeing him everywhere, in every face, was the desperate act of a woman praying her very own cowboy would ride in on his white horse and bring her to her senses.

Only problem with that scenario was that Cash not only didn't own a white horse, but no matter how much she craved her own wildly romantic ending, she was grounded enough in reality to know her leaving was the right decision.

JUST TO THE LEFT OF TULSA International's Starbucks, Cash tugged his best straw hat over his eyes. Had he not seen Wren taking his baby and his dog for himself, he might not have believed they were really leaving.

He wasn't supposed to be driving and he sure as hell wasn't supposed to be fawning over a woman who obviously loved her damned job more than him, but he couldn't help it. Wren had gotten under his skin, and until he discovered a way to exorcise her from his system, he'd have to throw himself into his work. He'd have to push himself harder. Ride as if there was no tomorrow. Because without Wren and Robin and even little Prissy in his life, there might as well not even be a tomorrow.

Solely so she could be a big-city doctor, Wren had broken his heart. And from where he stood, he doubted all the fancy degreed doctors in the world would be able to fix it.

"WHAT DO YOU MEAN WREN'S gone?" Georgina stood with her hands on her hips in Cash's home gym, staring at him as if he'd sprouted horns and a tail. "Like on a shopping trip to Tulsa?"

"No, Mom. Like in she moved back to Baltimore." It'd been forty-eight hours since his bride had vacated the premises and as far as he was concerned, Cash preferred to never speak of her again.

"Why'd you let her go? She didn't take Robin, did she?

What about the dog? Even a runt dog like Prissy needs fresh air and plenty of country to roam around in."

"Look…" He stopped his workout and grabbed a nearby water bottle. "Long story short, she felt her work was more important than me—or the rest of her family and friends. End of story."

"Well, what are you doing here?" his mom demanded. "Go after her. Drag her back caveman-style if you have to, but get her back."

He rolled his eyes.

"You think I'm kidding? Any fool could see the girl's crazy about you. And no grandchild of mine needs to be growing up without her daddy."

Easing up from his weight bench, Cash tossed a towel around his neck and limped to his gym's door.

"Don't ignore me, son. I've been on this earth a lot longer than you and recognize true love when I see it."

Cash snorted. "You must need a new eyeglasses prescription, because where me and Wren are concerned, there never was much between us but lust."

ONE MONTH LATER WREN SAT alone, save for Prissy, at a mahogany dining-room table large enough to seat twenty. Exhausting work hours had forced her to wean Robin so that the nanny Abigail had found could bottle-feed her.

It was ten at night, and she'd been home only fifteen minutes. Just long enough to peek in on her baby, grab a quick shower and scoop up her dog.

The housekeeper had informed her that Abigail and her significant other were at a fundraiser and not expected home until late. Mrs. Rodriguez had then warmed Wren a pasta-and-chicken dish that was too heavy on olive oil and garlic to suit her taste. What she could use was a big slice of Mrs. Cahwood's meat loaf with sides of green beans and buttery mashed potatoes.

Wren offered Prissy, who occupied her lap, a pea-sized bite of chicken, but the dog took one whiff of the pretentious food and went back to sleep.

Picking out the tomatoes and nibbling on somewhat edible garlic toast, Wren wondered for the umpteenth time what she was doing with her life. She hadn't wanted to be in research, but to heal people. Granted, because of her pregnancy she'd been forced out of her current year of residency, but might she have been better off staying at the ranch until July?

Living with Abigail, she'd managed to save enough money for her own place, but her friend had insisted she and the baby stay. After all, it wasn't as if their paths crossed that often in the rambling estate.

She'd sent apology letters to Georgina and her friends. She'd also packed her mother-in-law's Kewpie doll in a tissue-lined box, returning it with a note of thanks. So far she'd received only short, sharp notes from Mrs. Cahwood and Delores, imploring her to return home.

But had the ranch ever truly been her home? Had she ever in her life had a genuine home outside the fantasy image she carried in her mind?

The one where she wouldn't have met Cash until she'd been well finished with her residency. The one where she certainly wouldn't have had a child until she could afford to take off enough time to be with her.

As it was, what had Wren accomplished besides

being lonely and bored with every aspect of her life, with nothing but memories of happier times?

"YOU EVER GOING TO GO get her?" Dallas asked Cash one early-spring afternoon when it seemed as if every blooming thing in the world was coming alive save for him. They'd been riding fences, and had yet to find one in need of repair. Cash figured his brother just wanted an excuse to not only get him out of the house, but nag his little brother.

"If by *her*, you're referring to my wife," Cash said, "then nope."

"Mom told me what a screwed-up childhood Wren had. Think she might need lessons on the meaning of love?"

Frowning, Cash asked, "Isn't it a little early in the day for you to be hitting the bottle?"

"I'm serious. If I could have Bobbie Jo back for just a minute, I sure as hell wouldn't waste it fighting. Your woman and child and even your dog are just a few states east. All you have to do is fly over there and get 'em."

"Yup." Cash spotted a loose place in the fence and reined in his mount to climb off and set about fixing it.

"Then why don't you?" Already down from his horse, Dallas reached into his saddlebag for a hammer and nails.

"What don't you get about the fact that she left me? My knee's getting better by the day and I'm already in talks to head back out on the road. I'm a hot commodity and I'll be damned if I let some woman determine my self-worth."

"Been watching much of those daytime talk shows?"

his brother asked with a chuckle. "You're starting to sound like that Oprah."

"Oh, yeah? Well, you sound like a pain in my ass."

"I'M SORRY," WREN'S supervisor said over the phone Thursday morning, "but with patient trials starting, I can't spare you today."

"My infant daughter has a 103-degree fever," she explained. "I don't feel comfortable leaving her with a nanny."

Nathaniel cleared his throat. "I don't mean to be rude, but isn't that the whole point of hiring a nanny? So that parents don't have to be inconvenienced by these things?"

"These *things?*" Wren tried slow breathing to keep from blowing her cool, but failed miserably. "We're talking about my baby girl. As a doctor, didn't you take an oath that warmth, sympathy and understanding may outweigh the surgeon's knife or the chemist's drug?"

"Pollyanna," her boss said in a snide tone, "when you get a chance to fly back to reality, give me a call. Until then, consider yourself on probation."

"Never mind," Wren said. "I quit." Pressing the off button on her cell, Wren should've been upset. But all she really felt was an enormous sense of relief.

Maybe she'd return to Baltimore to restart her residency in July or maybe not. One thing she was sure of was that when she did finally earn her license, she wouldn't do it at the expense of her daughter.

Taking Robin from her crib, she dismissed the nanny for the day and then sat in a rocker in front of the nursery's bay window. Singing a soft lullaby, stroking her daughter's downy hair, it occurred to Wren that this was the first time since leaving the ranch that the two of them had spent quality time together.

The fact not only shamed her, but empowered her.

For Wren's entire life she'd searched for family. For a career that made her feel needed and whole. She couldn't believe that once she'd finally found it all, she'd thrown it away. How many times had she sworn that when she had a child, she'd be different from her own parents? She'd never abandon him or her to be raised by strangers. But look what she'd gone and done. For all her certainty that returning to Baltimore was right for her, she'd never considered how incredibly wrong it was for Robin. In Weed Gulch her daughter had a father and doting grandmother and cousins and uncles. Living in this mausoleum, she had a full-time nanny and all the priceless objets d'art anyone could ever want. But when it came right down to it, this place wasn't a real home any more than Wren's orphanage.

Home had nothing to do with a roof, but the people residing under that roof. People who loved you and comforted you and made you feel whole. People like Cash—her *husband*. The man she loved with every breath in her body.

Wren might be highly educated, but when it came to common sense, she was sadly lacking.

Key word—*was*.

From here on out, no more putting work above family. Not only was she no longer afraid of giving her heart to others, but she'd found a new mission. One designed to win back the hearts of those whom she'd no doubt badly hurt.

Chapter Twenty

"As I live and breathe…" Delores held open her front door. "Get in here before all three of you catch your death of cold."

"Thanks." Teeth chattering, Robin and Prissy in her arms, Wren said, "I'd forgotten how Oklahoma wind can turn what would otherwise be a perfectly nice afternoon into a walk-in freezer."

"You've got that right." To the baby she said, "Look how she's grown. When she sees her, Georgina's going to bust with pride."

Though it'd been only a little more than five weeks since Wren had been gone, it felt like a lifetime. Had she been as brave as she'd felt back in Baltimore, demanding Abigail sign her transfer forms, she would have gone to the ranch before stopping anywhere else. As it was, Wren needed to test the waters. Hear from a trusted source whether or not she was even still welcome at the place she used to call home.

After ten agonizingly long minutes of small talk, Delores finally got around to the important stuff. "Much as it flatters me to think you missed me bad enough that I'm the first one in Weed Gulch you'd want to visit, I suspect the real reason you haven't yet been out to the ranch is you're wanting the inside scoop on how Cash and the rest of your kin took your leaving."

"H-how do you know I haven't been to the ranch?"

"Girl, you forget, nobody comes down this road without me knowing." Laughing and patting her thighs, she said, "How about you hand over that baby and then I'll tell you everything you want to know."

THIRTY MINUTES LATER Wren turned her powerful SUV, the first car she'd ever owned, down her home's drive. It was funny how she loved the freedom of finally having her own vehicle but no longer cared for sleeping alone.

Since quitting, then telling Abigail that just because she believed Wren was well suited for being the next cardiac superstar didn't mean that was the path she wanted to take, this was the first time she'd been without Robin or Prissy. Besides learning just how angry Cash was with her, Wren had also been in desperate need of Delores's services as a sitter. Should Cash decide not to give her a second chance, she didn't want their daughter witnessing the ugly scene.

As she approached the achingly familiar house, a knot formed in her throat she feared wouldn't soon go away.

After parking and exiting the car, she added a light tremble and upset stomach to her body's list of complaints.

She rang the doorbell, only to have no one answer.

A glance at her watch told her that by three in the afternoon, Mrs. Cahwood was long gone.

Worrying her lower lip, Wren looked to the barn, only to now lose all of her air. Exiting the corral was

Cash in all his cowboy glory. Walking tall with no sign of a limp, he wore his favorite cowboy hat, a dust-covered white T-shirt, faded jeans and those damned chaps that had first landed her in trouble all the way back in Vegas.

Never had she seen a more handsome man—or one whose expression looked more thunderous.

Pulse racing to a degree she'd never dreamed possible, her mouth summer-drought dry, Wren raised her chin and continued walking toward her husband. She wanted to run. Toss her arms around him and never let go. But in leaving, she'd given up that right and didn't blame him for his icy reception.

"Where's my baby?" he asked, his jaw hard and his normally welcoming green eyes icy-cold.

"Safe and happy with Delores. Prissy's there, too. If you don't mind, I'd like a few minutes on our own, not being parents, but a couple."

Gazing across rolling prairie, he said, "I've been thinking a lot about filing for divorce. If that's why you're here, I'd be the last person to stop you from making the death of our marriage official."

It crushed her to know the man she'd finally realized she loved thought so poorly of her. But in the same respect, learning he hadn't already taken it upon himself to draw up a legal separation was great news. That meant the door for reconciliation might not be wide open, but it also wasn't padlocked shut.

Forcing a breath, she managed to whisper, "I'm not here to divorce you, Cash, but confess how much I love you."

He tensed. "So help me, if this is some big-city game

designed to trick me into signing over my legal rights to Robin, I'll—"

Desperate to derail his negative train of thought, Wren used the only *trick* she knew. The one stemming from the sexual chemistry neither had ever been able to control.

Arms around his neck, she kissed him as if there was no tomorrow, because from where she stood, there might not be. She kissed him hard and softly and every way in between, not only hungry for his taste, but desperate for his understanding.

"I'm so sorry," she murmured between kisses. "My leaving was the most harebrained thing I've ever done. I had to, though, to prove to myself what we shared was real. A thousand times more important than some residency at a prestigious hospital. I no longer even want prestigious, but meaningful. I want what Doc Haven has—not just patients, but friends. I've already made calls, and my former dean promised to put in a good recommendation for me with OU. If all goes well, I'll start in Tulsa in July. It'll still be rough, being apart from you for even days, but the end prize will mean I could set up a practice right here in Weed Gulch. I even bought an SUV for just that reason. So that even in bad weather I'll be able to get to anyone who needs me."

"Woman," Cash noted, "you first showed up on my property talking a mile a minute and telling me how things were going to be. Well, hate to burst your bubble, but you wearing the pants in this relationship no longer works for me."

Terrified he was on the verge of telling her to climb back into her car and drive on out of his life, her fingertips turned numb.

"At the airport, watching you go, I knew you were making a huge mistake, but—"

"You were there?" Hand over her mouth, eyes tearing, she said, "I knew I saw you, but I thought my imagination was playing tricks on me."

"Oh…" He laughed. "I was there, all right, telling myself over and over about that old saying. You know the one? How if you love something, you have to set it free?"

Nodding and not bothering to hide her tears, she said, "If you'll have me, Cash, I'm back, and wanting nothing more than to be your wife."

"You just refuse to let me have the last word, don't you?"

He tried looking stern, but his scowl transformed into the grin that had never failed to turn her tummy upside down. "Robin will always be welcome, but if I'm going to let you and your silly little dog back into my bed, there are going to be changes."

"Whatever you'd like." Dizzy with relief even though she still had Georgina's wrath to face, Wren was more than willing to make a few concessions.

"First," he said, holding her tight while kissing the crown of her head, "well, second after I get my hands on our gorgeous baby for a nice long hug, we're going on a proper honeymoon. You teased me back in Vegas and then here, prancing around in your pregnant glory…"

Now she was laughing. "I would hardly call my blimplike shape glorious."

"Trust me, it was. And I've been horny for you for months. Third, you ever so much as think about leaving me again, I want it in writing that I have permission to lasso you to the bed."

"Done," she said, warm and shivery at the thought of him once again having his cowboy way with her.

"Finally—and this one's a biggie—you will have to tell me on a daily basis that I'm the most handsome man you've ever seen, ever hope to see and will *ever* see. Think that's something you can manage?"

Laughing and crying at the same time, Wren whole-heartedly agreed.

* * * * *

Look for Laura Marie Altom's next book set on the prairie of Oklahoma and find out who catches Dallas Buckhorn—and tames his mischievous twins!
THE RANCHER'S TWIN TROUBLES

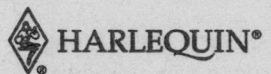

HARLEQUIN®

COMING NEXT MONTH

Available January 11, 2011

#1337 COLORADO COWBOY
American Romance's Men of the West
C.C. Coburn

#1338 RAMONA AND THE RENEGADE
Forever, Texas
Marie Ferrarella

#1339 THE BACHELOR RANGER
Creature Comforts
Rebecca Winters

#1340 THE WEDDING BARGAIN
Here Comes the Bride
Lee McKenzie

REQUEST YOUR FREE BOOKS!
2 FREE NOVELS PLUS 2 FREE GIFTS!

HARLEQUIN®

American Romance®

Love, Home & Happiness!

HARLEQUIN®

A *Romance*

FOR EVERY MOOD™

Spotlight on

— Classic —

Quintessential, modern love stories
that are romance at its finest.

**See the next page
to enjoy a sneak peek from
the Harlequin Presents® series.**

CATCLASSHP11

Harlequin Presents® is thrilled
to introduce the first installment of
an epic tale of passion and drama by
USA TODAY *Bestselling Author*
Penny Jordan!

*When buttoned-up Giselle first meets
the devastatingly handsome Saul Parenti,
the heat between them is explosive....*

"LET ME GET THIS STRAIGHT. Are you actually suggesting that I would stoop to that kind of game playing?"

Saul came out from behind his desk and walked toward her. Giselle could smell his hot male scent and it was making her dizzy, igniting a low, dull, pulsing ache that was taking over her whole body.

Giselle defended her suspicions. "You don't want me here."

"No," Saul agreed, "I don't."

And then he did what he had sworn he would not do, cursing himself beneath his breath as he reached for her, pulling her fiercely into his arms and kissing her with all the pent-up fury she had aroused in him from the moment he had first seen her.

Giselle certainly *wanted* to resist him. But the hand she raised to push him away developed a will of its own and was sliding along his bare arm beneath the sleeve of his shirt, and the body that should have been arching away from him was instead melting into him.

Beneath the pressure of his kiss he could feel and taste her gasp of undeniable response to him. He wanted to devour her, take her and drive them both until they were equally satiated—even whilst the anger within him that she should make him feel that way roared and burned its resentment of his need.

She was helpless, Giselle recognized, totally unable to withstand the storm lashing at her, able only to cling to the man who was the cause of it and pray that she would survive.

Somewhere else in the building a door banged. The sound exploded into the sensual tension that had enclosed them, driving them apart. Saul's chest was rising and falling as he fought for control; Giselle's whole body was trembling.

Without a word she turned and ran.

Find out what happens when Saul and Giselle succumb to their irresistible desire in

THE RELUCTANT SURRENDER

Available January 2011 from Harlequin Presents®

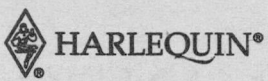

HARLEQUIN®

American ★ Romance®

C.C. COBURN
Colorado Cowboy

American Romance's
Men of the West

It had been fifteen years since Luke O'Malley,
divorced father of three, last saw his high school
sweetheart, Megan Montgomery. Luke is shocked to
discover they have a son, Cody, a rebellious teen on his
way to juvenile detention. The last thing either of them
expected was nuptials. Will these strangers rekindle
their love or is the past too far behind them?

**Available January
wherever books are sold.**

"LOVE, HOME & HAPPINESS"

www.eHarlequin.com

har75341

ROMANTIC
SUSPENSE

Sparked by Danger, Fueled by Passion.

Cowboy Deputy
by
CARLA CASSIDY

Following a run of bad luck, including an attack on her grandfather, Edie Tolliver is sure things can't possibly get any worse....

But with the handsome Deputy Grayson on the case will Edie's luck and love life turn a corner?

LAWMEN
of BLACK ROCK

Available January 2011
wherever books are sold.

Visit Silhouette Books at www.eHarlequin.com

SRS27709